OR 11-11

D1020947

Carina laid her hea[...]d
concentrated on the [...]
Bishop's caring gaze.

He had seemed worried, as if he truly cared about her. But how could that be possible? Hadn't he shown the same compassion for Abel?

She stood and walked back to the window, feeling a bit stronger. Susan had told her how much her son had changed in the time he'd been gone. How becoming a Christian had changed him from a selfish, spoiled boy to a gentle, caring man. Leaning her head against the window frame, she wondered if that was true. Was Susan just a proud mother, overemphasizing her son's positive traits?

Betsey's labored footsteps plodded down the hall in her direction. Could she talk to her about Dr. Bishop? She heaved a sigh. Probably not. Her maid had fallen in love with him the day he splinted Abel's leg, and now Betsey's feelings had surely grown like bread dough on a warm day since he'd taken such good care of her.

Rather than dreading her next encounter with Reed Bishop, she looked forward to it. Was there any hope they might become friends? Was she willing to turn loose of her bitterness to make that happen?

Even if she did, how could he ever forget how she had treated him?

And what about Johan? Could it possibly be true her brother had started the duel?

She shook her head. She didn't have a prayer of a chance that a Zimmer and a Bishop could ever make peace.

VICKIE McDONOUGH believes God is the ultimate designer of romance. She is a wife of thirty-six years, mother to four grown sons, and a doting grandma. When not writing, she enjoys reading, watching movies, and traveling. Visit Vickie's website at www.vickiemcdonough.com.

Books by Vickie McDonough

Dueling
Hearts

Vickie McDonough

Heartsong Presents

This book is dedicated to Barbour and the staff who work there. I wouldn't have a writing career if not for Barbour, and I will always be grateful to Becky Germany for buying that first novella and the ones that followed and then later for acquiring my first trade fiction series. Thank you, Tracie Peterson, for seeing something good in my writing and purchasing my first four Heartsong books and to Joanne Simmons for buying the next seven. Thanks also to the folks behind the scenes who work so diligently to put out a good product.

A note from the Author:
I love to hear from my readers! You may correspond with me by writing:

Vickie McDonough
Author Relations
PO Box 721
Uhrichsville, OH 44683

ISBN 978-1-61626-539-7

DUELING HEARTS

All scripture quotations are taken from the King James Version of the Bible.

This book is a work of fiction. Names, characters, places, and incidents are either products of the author's imagination or used fictitiously.

Our mission is to publish and distribute inspirational products offering exceptional value and biblical encouragement to the masses.

PRINTED IN THE U.S.A.

one

Charleston, South Carolina
1848

"Who is that lovely black-eyed Susan hiding behind the potted plants?" Reed Bishop nodded his head toward the corner of the large ballroom where a dark-haired nymph leaned against the wall, head down.

Damian squinted, staring past the stringed quartet, and shrugged. "She's a pretty thing, although that yellow dress of hers is rather shabby." He lifted his glass and sipped the punch, eyeing the young woman with disdain.

"Hmm. . . Maybe the gown looks shabby because her loveliness outshines it."

Damian sputtered then started coughing. When he regained his composure, he glanced at Reed with glistening eyes. "Are you turning poetic?"

Reed looked away, not wanting his friend to think he was besotted. He stared at the woman for another long moment then tugged his gaze toward the colorful line of dancers sashaying to the lively music.

"Why don't you ask her to dance?"

Reed shrugged. He probably would, but he didn't want Damian thinking it had been his idea.

"How did you manage to sit this round out, anyway? All the ladies have been chasing after you, anxious to catch your eye before you leave town."

Reed pursed his lips. "Mother pulled me aside to introduce me to an old friend, and the music had already started when we finished talking."

"Well, if I were you, I'd have snagged one of them gals anyhow."

"I can't say I don't enjoy the attention, but I feel kind of like a treed coon at times."

Damian grinned. "If you feel that way now, just wait until you return from college as a surgeon."

Huffing a laugh, Reed failed to see the lure. "Most surgeons don't have two half dimes to rub together."

His friend nudged Reed in the arm and winked. "Most surgeons aren't the grandson of Cooper Reed and half owner of Reed Shipping, and most don't own a plantation as large and prosperous as Reed Springs." Damian shook his head. "Why do you insist on sailing off to the wilds of Scotland when you have a thriving business to run here?"

Shifting his gaze back to the sprite in the corner, Reed shrugged. He hated it when one of his friends pointed out his family's wealth. He had the fortune—and oft times, misfortune—to be born into a wealthy family, but he didn't want people befriending him for that reason alone. Damian was his best friend, but he had never understood Reed's interest in science and didn't want him going away for several years. There was no point trudging through that muck again.

"I'm halfway surprised that your mother didn't keep you at home today, seeing as how you set sail in the morning. Is she still trying to get you to change your mind?"

He watched Dudley Brown approach the young woman in the yellow dress. "Yes, she doesn't understand my love for science and my preference to become a surgeon rather than running the plantation."

"You're her only son. It's expected you'd follow in your father's footsteps."

"My cousin is better suited to run Reed Shipping—and he has the desire."

Dudley Brown placed one hand on the wall to the right of the woman's shoulder and leaned toward her. The sprite's eyes widened, and her head swiveled back and forth like a weather vane in a thunderstorm. Reed grinned, glad she had the sense to refuse a rascal like Dudley. What would she say if *he* asked her to take a spin with him? He took a step in her direction.

"Good luck!" Damian called out.

As he drew closer, Reed sensed there was something familiar about the girl. Her eyes—as dark as black coffee—widened when he stopped a proper distance away. Her thin eyebrows dipped, and her mouth puckered. Hardly the response Reed expected—even worse than when Dudley had approached her.

"Good afternoon. I hope you're having a nice time here."

"I was doin' fine till *you* arrived." She turned her head away and stared over the leaves of a small palm tree toward the open doors to the veranda.

Not used to being snubbed by a Southern woman, Reed was taken off guard. Had he offended her somehow? But how could that be possible when he didn't think he'd even met her before? He glanced back at Damian. His friend eyed him with obvious curiosity. Reed hated to fail, especially when a friend was watching. "Have we met previously?"

She stiffened, hiking up her chin and staring at him with those captivating eyes. Had he ever seen a fair-skinned woman with eyes the color of onyx before?

"I can't believe you'd ask me that," she snapped at him, like an alligator latching on to its dinner.

He grappled for a response, but before he could form a retort, she darted between the potted trees and ran out the door.

Damian hurried toward him. "The only other time I've ever seen a female run away from you was the time you kissed the preacher's daughter right after church last Easter. What in the world did you say to that girl?"

"Nothing." Reed's arms hung limp at his side, and he held out his hands. "Nothing at all. She seemed to think she knew me, but I've never met her before."

"She must have confused you with someone else."

Reed shrugged. The venom she spat at him had purpose. He may not have known her, but he was certain she knew him.

Clapping him on the shoulder, Damian gave Reed a gentle shake. "Don't fret over her. There are plenty of other butterflies in the garden you can cast your net over."

"Ha! Who's waxing poetic now?"

His friend's hazel eyes twinkled, and his ears turned red. "My cup is empty. How about joining me for some more punch?"

Reed followed, but his gaze clung to the doorway where the confusing woman had fled. He'd never had a woman run away from him before—at least not one without a justifiable reason—and it intrigued him. Most times women competed for his attention, batting their long lashes at him and even pushing their friends out of the way to get closer to him. He knew he was handsome—and wealthy—and he had the striking blue eyes that many of the Reed men he'd descended from had— eyes that women found irresistible. All but this woman.

❧

Carina raced down the hall, hoping against hope that *he* didn't follow. Her stomach churned just to be standing so close to a Bishop. And to think she'd actually talked to him. Not that she'd been very pleasant.

But he had surprised her. She'd never imagined *he* would ask her to dance.

Clenching her fist, she swung her arms as she marched in a quite unladylike fashion down the upstairs hall to the room she'd gotten dressed in earlier. Reed Bishop's blue eyes haunted her thoughts. And until she'd seen him up close, she hadn't realized how his thick hair resembled the color of her favorite cypress swing on her front porch. She'd be lying if she denied he was handsome. Too bad that he knew it and used his charm to attract females. Every other woman might beg him to dance and swoon at his feet, but she sure never would. Not ever.

She all but ran into the bedchamber where she had dressed earlier and dropped down onto the dressing table chair. She stared at her reflection in the mirror. Her hair, which she'd attempted to fashion into something pretty this morning, now listed to the left like a sinking ship. Yanking out the pins, she shook her head, and her locks tumbled past her shoulders, down her back. There was no point in trying to look like a lady. She failed miserably. Her dress looked like a worn-out slave's garment compared to the other gowns in the ballroom. Oh, why had she allowed Betsey to talk her into coming? She didn't belong here.

Tossing aside the finer travel bags stacked in the corner, she located her ragged satchel in the back, as if someone had been trying to hide it. Tugging hard, she pulled it free and fell back. She flung out her arm, whacking it against the tall post of the bed. Spinning sideways, she landed in a heap on the floor, with her skirt over her head.

In spite of everything, she started laughing. At least no one had seen her clumsy acrobatics. She pulled her skirt and petticoat off her face, and her gaze landed on a wide-eyed servant standing in the doorway.

The woman blinked several times then found her voice. "You. . .ah. . .be needin' some he'p, miz?"

two

Reed was ready for the lengthy Virginia reel to be over so he could dance with a pretty girl and forget the sassy black-eyed Susan. His mind raced, searching every nook and cranny of his brain, trying to figure out why the woman had been so terse with him. He kept coming back to the same conclusion: she must have confused him with someone else, as Damian had suggested.

As the lovely ladies sidestepped past him on their way back to the front of the line where they'd meet their partners and then duck under the clasped hands of the lead couple, several of the unmarried women winked or smiled at him. Which one had he promised the next dance to?

The image of the female who had snubbed him entered his mind again. He wouldn't be content until he tracked her down and got the truth from her. He spun on his heel and strode toward the door where she'd exited the ballroom.

"Bishop! Ree' Bishop!"

Upon hearing his name shouted so rudely from across the room, Reed stopped and pivoted around. A ruckus to his right pulled his gaze back to the center of the room. The dancers skidded to a halt and looked around. Loud mumbles arose, and the couples in the center of the room stumbled aside as a man pushed his way through them. Many folks watched the man, but others turned and stared at Reed.

Damian hurried to his side. "Who is that?"

Reed shook his head, searching the crowd for his mother.

He had no desire for her to be embarrassed in front of her friends by a man he must have upset somehow. The man staggered through the last of the dancers, and the music squeaked to a halt. The buzz of speculation filled the room like disturbed bees.

"Isn't that Johan Zimmer?" Damian asked. "Looks like he's chugged full."

Reed's gut twisted. He hadn't seen the Zimmers in years, in spite of the fact they were among his nearest neighbors. Not since. . .

Johan stopped three feet from Reed. "Yer fam'ly. . .they are c—cause of all our troubles." Johan swiped his sleeve across his mouth and took several quick steps back before he regained his balance, such as it was. Even from four feet away, Reed could smell the liquor on the man's breath. The Bishops and the Zimmers rarely socialized in the same circles. Johan was half a foot taller than Reed remembered but still as thin as a ship's ratline.

Damian glanced sideways at Reed, brows lifted. From across the room, Reed saw Mr. Hanover, the host of the ball, and several other men moving along the edge of the crowd toward them, probably thinking to stop a fight.

But a fight was the last thing Reed wanted. He'd thought the Zimmers' anger over what had happened had finally died down now that Karl Zimmer had been injured and had taken to his bed. Johan's father had been the one to stir up things when Reed's father was still alive, but since his death, the Zimmers had been quiet.

Damian stepped forward, his hand outstretched. He laid it on Johan's shoulder. "This isn't the place for a personal squabble, Zimmer."

Sloughing off Damian's hand, Johan scowled and staggered

sideways, sloshing the wine in his glass onto the floor. Miss Abigail DuPree, who stood on Johan's far side, squealed and back stepped, holding up the skirt of her pink gown. She frowned at him, then pivoted and pushed her way through the gawking crowd.

Oblivious, Johan held out his bony finger. "I d'mand justice. Your *fader*, he cheated my f–fader, out of wha' was righ'fully his."

Reed stiffened and closed the space between him and Johan. "That's a lie, and you know it, as well as everyone else in this room."

Johan jerked as if he'd been slapped, splashing red wine onto his white shirt. "You have in–in–insulted a Zimmer for the las' time, Ree' Bishop." Johan tucked his wine under his arm, spilling the last of the liquid. He struggled to pull a glove from his waistband—a glove that looked closer to gray than white. Finally gaining hold, he yanked out the glove and slapped it to the ground at Reed's feet. "I ch–challenge you to a d–duel."

Gasps rippled across the room. Reed clenched his jaw. The dueling *Code of Honor* stated that a gentleman should never challenge another gentleman to a duel in public. That this man had, further insulted Reed.

Mr. Hanover drew up beside him. "You gentlemen take this disagreement outside. I'll not have dissension in my home."

"I apologize for this disturbance, sir," Reed said.

Mr. Hanover gave him a long, hard stare then nodded. Spinning on his heel, Reed glanced at the door where the woman in the faded yellow dress had fled. Maybe he'd see her later and could question her then.

He strode out the open double doors, past the silent, gawking string quartet, and onto the piazza. He clenched his fist as he passed several strolling couples out to the lawn and waited. Why, after years of silence, would Johan Zimmer choose today to once again accuse his father? Would these verbal attacks never end? His family had lost far more than the Zimmers when that cargo ship sank in a storm seven years ago. Johan couldn't have been more than ten years old then, so what had stirred him up to feel the need to force a duel?

With hands on hips, Reed watched Johan stumble down the stairs, nearly falling to his knees before righting himself. He searched for Reed, then his gaze latched onto him, and he proceeded forward, with a crowd of curious spectators following.

Reed had no desire to duel Johan. It would hardly be a fair battle anyway, with the man more than half drunk. But his own honor—and more so, his father's—had been insulted in front of their closest friends and business associates. To back down would belittle him in the eyes of the many men present who had dealings with Reed Shipping. And how would his mother look upon his participation? He heaved a loud sigh. There was no way he could win this ordeal.

He expected to see his mother leading the spectators. She would call a halt to the duel if she had it in her power—and profoundly embarrass him in the process. If he was fortunate, prior to Johan's disturbance she had left the ballroom to take an afternoon respite as some of the older women had and was not yet aware of the situation. He ran his hand through his hair. He should have stayed home and finished packing, but no, he had to have one last day of enjoyment before facing years of study.

Johan tottered to a stop several feet away and glared at him.

Damian hurried past him to Reed's side. "I'll serve as your second."

Reed leaned toward him. "I can't duel him in the condition he's in."

"People will think you're a coward if you don't. Besides, you don't have to shoot the man—just fire off to his side. Then his honor should be satisfied."

"And what if he shoots me?"

"Look at him. He couldn't hit the broad side of a clipper ship if he was ten paces away. How do you expect him to hit you?"

"Maybe he'll miss and shoot you instead."

Damian's eyes widened and he grinned, but Reed could see that his comment had shaken his friend. "Maybe I'll just go stand behind that tree over there."

Reed chuckled in spite of everything.

"Johan doesn't have the guts to go through with a duel," Damian said.

Tucker Marlow squeezed through the crowd and jogged toward Reed, a wooden box held tight under his arm. The man had supervised more duels in Charleston than anyone Reed knew.

Damian stepped back, and Marlow stopped where he'd been standing.

"Come over here, Mr. Zimmer." Tucker waved his fingers, beaconing Reed's accuser to join them.

Johan stumbled forward, his eyes dropping to the box. Uncertainty flickered in his eyes before his gaze hardened. Johan had always been a quiet boy, from the little Reed could remember about him. His father, though, had been vocal about his perceived wrong, in spite of the fact that everyone knew sending a shipload of cargo across the ocean was always a gamble. Reed's father might have owned the ship with Zimmer's harvest onboard, but it was hardly his fault the vessel had sunk in a storm.

Tucker cleared his throat. "Mr. Hanover has been kind enough to lend us the use of his dueling pistols, unless you prefer to use swords." He turned slightly to face Johan. "Mr. Zimmer, according to *The Code of Honor*, penned by our former governor John Lyde Wilson, you may apologize and walk away from this duel with your honor intact. Do you wish to offer Mr. Bishop an apology?"

Reed prayed the man had the sense to express regret for the way he'd slandered the Bishop family name and Reed's father. He had no desire to duel a drunken man.

Tugging at one earlobe, Johan glanced at Reed then at the crowd of spectators. He scowled. "He c–called me a liar, and his fader was a—a cheat. It's time those B–Bishops paid for ruinin' us."

Heaving a sigh, Reed turned to his second. "I thought you said he didn't have the backbone to go through with this duel."

Damian waved his hand in the air. "I doubt he even knows how to shoot. He's always been a milksop."

"Maybe *I* should just apologize." A myriad of thoughts raced through Reed's mind. If he offered an apology for the things that had happened in the past, would Johan be satisfied? His honor restored? The Zimmers had blamed the Bishops for their misfortune for as long as Reed could remember. But apologizing for something he had no part in stuck in his craw. Expressing regret was difficult enough for a man when he was the guilty party. Besides, he was from a long line of patriots and backing down had never been an option.

He stood straighter and eyed the scrolling inscription etched on the box of dueling pistols. Reed didn't doubt his own skill with a pistol, and dueling was a commonly accepted form of settling disputes among Southern gentlemen, but was he ready to risk his life for the sake of his pride?

"Don't back down, Bishop. Everyone'll think you're yellow."

Reed glanced over his shoulder at Grady Howard, one of his future college classmates. Had the man actually read his thoughts?

Beside Grady stood another half-dozen men his age from wealthy families of the South, all of whom were leaving on the ship with him tomorrow. If he apologized now, they would all think him a coward. His reputation would be in shambles, and his classmates would make the years in Scotland miserable. There was no option left, but to continue. He turned his attention on his opponent and shook his head. "My family's honor has been ground into the dirt one time too many. It ends here. Today."

Johan's lips puckered, and his bloodshot eyes narrowed. "You Bishops don't know wha' honor is." He waved a hand at Tucker. "Get on with it."

"Do you have a second?" Tucker asked.

Johan looked around, as if hunting a friend. A man Reed didn't recognize stepped forward. "I'll be his second."

"Very well," Tucker said. He opened the box of dueling pistols and motioned for Reed's and Johan's seconds to step forward. "Mr. Bishop, as the wronged party, your second may choose first." Damian eyed the identical weapons then selected one. Both seconds loaded powder and ball; then each returned to his principal's side.

Reed eyed the pistol—a beautiful Henry Le Page creation with a walnut stock and a chrome-and-satin barrel. "Let me see it."

Damian handed over the pistol. Reed held it in his left hand, testing its weight, liking the feel of it in his hand. The firearm was a fine weapon and would serve him well.

Damian patted Reed's shoulder then took back the pistol. "I sure hope you come out the winner. I'd hate to lose my best friend. Having you go away for years is bad enough."

Reed swallowed the lump building in his throat. He could actually die today—and at just nineteen, dying was not something he'd wasted much time thinking about. Should he be the loser and perish, his mother would be shocked and deeply saddened that her only child was gone. They might not agree on many things, but he knew she loved him.

Tucker closed the pistol box and stepped forward. "Gentlemen, if you two will stand back-to-back, we'll get this thing over with."

Suddenly stiff and somber, Johan turned around and faced the other direction. Reed stalked over and stood behind him, the pistol in his hand shaking. He forced his fist to hold steady and inhaled a deep breath.

"All right, then, I will begin counting. You will both take a step in the opposite direction on each count I call out; then on number eight, you will turn and fire. God be with you both and may He vindicate the man in the right."

A trickle of sweat ran down Reed's temple. Off to his right, he recognized the chirp of a brown-headed nuthatch that flittered among the limbs of a tall pine tree. The bird's cheery squeaking was in dramatic contrast to the solemn event taking place on the massive lawn. The midafternoon sun struggled to peek through the gray clouds overhead, as if it, too, wanted to watch the events. In a paddock to his right, a dozen horses grazed peacefully on thick, green grass, and on the left, most of the spectators stood a respectable distance away. He couldn't help wondering which man they were cheering for. His family was well respected, but there were always those who despised them for their wealth and success.

"One."

Reed hesitated a moment then stepped forward when he felt Johan do so. He had only wanted to have an enjoyable day before he left America. Why couldn't Johan have kept silent?

"Two."

His whole body jarred as he paced forward. He swallowed the lump building in his throat. What a waste his life had been. His parents had coddled him and let him have his way much of the time when he was young. He'd grown into a young man who liked getting what he wanted.

"Three."

Five more steps to death, maiming, or vindication. But vindicating what? Would winning the duel actually restore honor to either man? Maybe in the eyes of those attending, but would it put an end to the Zimmers' accusations?

"Four."

Reed could no longer hear his opponent's heavy breathing. Was the man more sure of his abilities than he looked? A better shot than his reputation claimed him to be? Or maybe he was only pretending to be drunk. Reed clenched his jaw. He wasn't ready to die.

"Five."

Up to this point, he'd lived mostly for fun and for doing scientific research. He had preferred spending time in a tavern with his friends to working on the estate or at the shipping yard on the harbor that his father half owned. He remembered attending church when he was younger, but like his close friends, he hadn't seen a need for God or religion. He looked up at the sky. Would he stand face-to-face with God today?

"Six."

No, he wasn't ready. He had too much life to live. He'd

finally settled on a career that sounded halfway interesting. He couldn't die today. He'd never become a doctor. And yet, how could he become a doctor knowing he'd killed or maimed a neighbor?

"Seven."

If he allowed Johan the first shot, he could well die without ever firing his pistol. He pursed his lips. He couldn't kill the man; that much he knew. When he turned, he would delay firing and allow Johan the first shot; then he'd place a shot close enough to look real. If he perished, so be it, but at least he'd die with a clear conscience, knowing he hadn't taken advantage of a drunken man.

"Eight. Fire at will."

three

Carina stood on the expansive front porch of the Hanover home, waiting for the groom to locate her carriage and driver. She was so ready to head home. She never should have come. If only Betsey hadn't refashioned one of her mother's old gowns and encouraged her that attending today's ball would help her to get to know her neighbors better. But the slave woman was mistaken. The fine ladies of Charleston had made little to no effort to get to know her. They'd taken one look at her dress and stuck their rich noses up in the air. She was not a native of Charleston or even America. How could she ever hope to fit in with the local society?

No matter. She didn't need their friendship.

Leaning against a tall porch pillar, she studied the perfectly manicured lawn. The road leading up to the main entrance of her family's home looked like a forest compared to the Hanover's well-trimmed lawn and gardens. Farther away, dozens of palmettos lined both sides of the drive, making an inviting first view of the Hanover home. If she had forty-eight hours in a day, maybe hers could look as nice. At least she was able to file away several ideas for the day when she could squeeze out time to garden.

The door behind her opened, and Miss Elizabeth Hanover and two friends exited. They cast her an odd glance then sat in the rockers along the parlor window. Carina watched them out of the corner of her eye. All three were probably only a year or two younger than she. What would it be like to be friends with girls her own age? But then, those spoiled rich girls had nothing in common with her.

The young women giggled, and Elizabeth caught Carina's gaze. "I'm surprised to see you out here, considering what's happening out back."

Carina jerked her gaze away. Her cheeks warmed at the thought that the women had caught her staring at them. She glanced down the long drive, but her carriage still wasn't in sight. Then her mind latched onto what Elizabeth had said, and she turned back to face her. "What's going on out yonder?"

Elizabeth's blond brows lifted, and she glanced at her friends. "You mean you truly don't know?"

Carina shook her head.

"Oh, dear." The woman to Elizabeth's right lifted her fingertips to her lips.

Apprehension skittered up Carina's spine like ants climbing a tree. "What is it? And why would I be concerned?"

Elizabeth stood and walked toward her. "Your brother created quite a disturbance on the dance floor."

Scowling, Carina couldn't for the life of her imagine her highly introverted brother asking a woman to dance. He didn't even know how to dance, as far as she knew. Why, she had barely managed to get him to attend. She narrowed her eyes, not sure whether to believe the uppity woman or not. "What kind of disturbance?"

The woman in the lavender dress jumped up from her rocker and hurried to Elizabeth's side. "I thought it was so exciting. That Reed Bishop, he's so handsome and collected."

Carina's heart jolted. Hearing Reed Bishop's name mentioned in conjunction with her brother was not a good thing.

"We're not talking about Reed, Amanda." Elizabeth tossed

her head, and her blond ringlets bounced. She narrowed her eyes at Carina. "Your brother was drunk. He shouted across the ballroom, slandering Reed's father and disrupting the dance."

Carina felt the blood drain from her face. "What else happened?"

"Oh, Reed took it rather well, but your brother wouldn't listen and challenged him to a duel."

Carina gasped. "Today? Here?"

Both women nodded, but Elizabeth responded. "Yes, Reed leaves tomorrow to attend the Royal College of Physicians and Surgeons in Glasgow and will be gone several years. It had to be today."

Dropping her satchel, Carina picked up her skirts and raced across the porch and around the side of the house, her heart pounding. Her kindhearted brother knew little about weapons. He had no need for them since he couldn't stand to even squash a spider and thought hunting was cruel. He wouldn't even eat meat. Reed Bishop had been hunting all his life. She knew because she'd spied on him when she was younger. He was an expert shot and a man who had no heart. Her sweet brother was no match.

From the elevated porch, she could see across the wide, open lawn surrounded with pine trees on two sides, where many of the guests stood, watching the event. Farther past them, two men were already pacing away from one another. "No, no, no!"

She jogged down the steps, heedless of the heads turning her way. She had to stop this senseless battle.

With the crowd thinner along the edges, Carina squeezed her way past the wealthiest members of Charleston's society—past men and women dressed in their finery. Why would so many people, women especially, care to watch two men shooting at each other? Had they no sense of decency?

She had almost reached the edge of the crowd when she heard the counting.

"Six."

Relief almost slowed her steps. She wasn't too late. Didn't the count go to ten? "Move out of the way." She tried to go around, but the crowd was pressed up against a row of thick hedges that lined the side of the garden. Pushing between two giants, she heard the count of seven. "Let me pass. Please!"

One man glanced down and turned enough that she could squeeze past him. Finally she had a clear view of her brother and that horrible Reed Bishop.

"Eight. Fire at will."

"Nooo!" Carina screamed. She rushed toward her brother, but someone grabbed her from behind, jerking her backward. "Let me go! Please!"

The hands held firm.

❧

Reed spun around, holding his pistol in front of him. Johan stumbled around, waving his firearm in the air. Reed slowly lowered his. How could he shoot a man who couldn't even stand up straight?

To his left, a woman's scream pierced the air. Johan's pistol exploded. A moment later, Reed's left arm erupted with burning pain. He jumped, and his own pistol fired. He grabbed his arm and looked down. A slit had been sliced through the sleeve of his dress coat, and the camel-colored fabric was stained with crimson along the tear.

"Good show, Reed. How bad are you wounded?"

Shaken from his stupor, Reed stared at Damian. "I think he just winged me."

"Well, it looks like you did more than that to him."

Reed's gaze jerked back to where Johan had been standing. Remorse surged through him like a tidal wave. He'd shot Johan? He must have fired the gun when he jumped after getting shot. Johan lay on the ground, a mass of red covering his torso. A woman in a dark blue dress rushed to his side and fell to her knees in the grass. Shame gutted Reed. What had he done? "I wasn't going to shoot."

"Well you did, and you've been vindicated. Your honor is restored." Damian pried the pistol from his fingers. "Let me return this, and we'll get out of here before that wife of Johan's makes a scene."

Reed didn't feel very honorable. He didn't even know Johan had a wife. The crowd of spectators surged forward. Men clapped his uninjured shoulder, offering him their congratulations.

"Well done, Bishop."

"That's fine shooting."

"Expert marksmanship."

The praises floated around Reed's head like pesky flies. He had to get out of there before he was sick. Pushing through the crowd, he ignored the pain throbbing in his arm. He'd shot a man—and that man could die because of him. How could he become a doctor now that he had a man's blood on his hands?

four

Carina eyed the six slaves who stood by the wagon with
their heads hanging down. Each clung to a burlap bag that
held all of their belongings. She swallowed the aching lump
building in her throat. They were healthy and better dressed
than most slaves she'd seen in Charleston, and she knew each
one by name, knew how long they'd lived at Tanglewood.
Leasing them out was one of the hardest things she'd ever
done, but she had to have income, and she had few options
left. Tears burned her eyes, and she forced them away lest
Mr. Davies see her crying and attempt to take advantage
of her.

Most folks didn't give a hoot about their slaves and thought
of them only as property, but to Carina, they were her
friends—people she'd grown fond of and felt it her duty to
watch over. But she'd failed them, and choosing who to lease
to work in Charleston and who to keep was almost more than
she could bear. By leasing this half dozen for a short while, she
hoped to hang on to Tanglewood so that they would one day
be able to return. Tonight, when she was alone in her bed, she'd
cry at the unfairness of it all.

Lifting her head, she held out the slaves' papers then waited
for Mr. Davies to look over them. "You promised you'd do
right by them, and I'll trust you're a man of your word."

He grunted but merely continued perusing the papers. "Where's your daddy? And why ain't he out here tendin' to this business?"

Carina worked hard not to flinch. If Mr. Davies knew that her fader had taken to his bed over a year ago, he'd offer her half what she knew the slaves were worth. "I am the one handling this sale. Are we doing business or not?"

He rolled up the papers then studied her with narrowed eyes. "Looks like ever'thing is in order here." He smacked the roll against his palm. "Why not just sell them to me? I'll give you one thousand dollars for the lot of them."

Unable to hold back her gasp, she straightened her back and narrowed her gaze. "You'll not be taking advantage of me, Mr. Davies. Jesse alone is worth that much. If you're not interested in leasing them, you can take your business elsewhere."

He worked his mouth as if chewing on a slice of jerky. Rubbing his whiskery jaw with the back of his hand, he glared at her through unusually small eyes the color of swamp water. "You drive a hard bargain, Miss Zimmer. Perhaps we could barter a deal that would benefit us both."

Her fader had warned her that Mr. Davies was a shrewd businessman, but she wouldn't allow him to ramrod her. "What kind of deal?"

His lazy gaze drifted down her body, lingering at the most inappropriate places. She shifted from one foot to the other, fighting the desire to flee to the creek and wash off. She pulled a small pistol from her skirt pocket and crossed her arms, holding up the weapon with her shooting hand, her message clear. "I'll take two hundred dollars per month with the first two months up front as you promised or nothing. Make up your mind. I've got work waiting."

He muttered a half snarl, half laugh, then shook his head.

"I'll give you one hundred fifty dollars per month and not a half cent more."

Carina's heart sank. She longed to keep her workers. Without them, the few slaves she had left would find it very difficult to manage everything that needed done around Tanglewood. But if she didn't get the money to pay the mortgage, she'd lose the land that she'd given her heart and soul for. She simply had to make this bargain today. She would never be able to work up her nerve to lease her people again. Her fader had taught her that sometimes the best way to seal a deal was to walk away. "Then good day to you, sir."

She turned her back to Mr. Davies and strode toward her servants.

Mr. Davies uttered a curse. "Now just hold your horses, missy. They said you was hard-nosed, but I didn't believe it."

Who had said she was hard-nosed? She turned back to face the despicable man, not at all liking that people had been talking about her.

"All right, I'll give you one hundred eighty dollars."

"The price is two hundred dollars. And you're getting a bargain."

He heaved a heavy sigh and shook his head. "All right. Two hundred dollars. But don't expect me to be coming around again to pay. You can come to Charleston to collect your payment."

Carina almost smiled at the relief she felt, in spite of knowing she'd have to travel so far to collect her money each month. Her fingers tingled as she watched him count out the bills and coins. She could pay the taxes and two mortgage payments, purchase some much-needed supplies and also seed for next spring's planting. And maybe now she could afford to hire a doctor from town to help her fader.

She kept the pistol in sight, counting the money as Mr. Davies did. He held it out like a man giving away his last dollar. She snatched it before he could change his mind. "Remember, it says in our agreement that you'll treat my people fairly, feed them well, and not beat them."

His thick lips tilted to one side, putting her in mind of a snarling wolf that had been in one too many fights. "They ain't *your people* for the time bein'. They belong to me now."

Her stomach clenched. Had she made a mistake? What other choice did she have? She'd already sold as much land as she could part with and still have a decent harvest. Fighting back more tears, she walked past each of the six Negroes who had served her so faithfully. "Thank you for your service here. I hope that this will be a temporary situation. Please work as hard for Mr. Davies as you would for me." She wanted to add *so he'll treat you well*, but she feared it wasn't true.

The four women in the group sniffled and offered her sympathetic glances before ducking their heads again. The two men didn't look up. She knew they understood she had no other choice, but they were frightened and filled with uncertainty about their futures.

Mr. Davies flicked his hand at the man who drove the big buckboard. "Isaac, get them Negroes on up in the back of that there wagon."

At Mr. Davies's harsh command, Carina spun around and hurried toward the house, the money in her hand feeling like thirty pieces of silver. She picked up her pace and jogged up the steps. She ran into the house, slammed the front door, and dashed up the stairs with tears racing down her cheeks. She'd always secretly hoped to set her slaves free one day. Buying, selling, and leasing was for produce and livestock, not people, and yet she was as guilty as the men she despised.

Hunger and desperation drove people to do things they wouldn't normally do.

In her bedroom, she hid the money in a false bottom drawer in her dressing table then fell on her bed, exhausted and heartbroken. She despised crying, but her tears flowed like a swollen river cresting its banks, and she couldn't do a thing about it.

Would the day ever come when she had someone to lean on?

She was so tired of being strong.

ଈ

A fog parted, and Carina strolled along the banks of the river. She should be working, she was certain, but the peacefulness beckoned her. The water swished and splashed gently against the rocks lining the bank, in tune with the songbirds in the thick greenery above her. Across the river, a huge alligator sunned itself in the warm afternoon. They were massive creatures, those 'gators, with few cares in the world except finding something to eat and avoiding hunters who'd kill them for their hide. Would this one end up a pair of boots on some wealthy planter's feet?

She sat on a sun-kissed stone and rested her elbows on her knees, chin in her hand. Here, away from her fader's glare and verbal rantings, she could be the young woman she dreamed of—one whose only worries were which dress she would wear to the ball next week or in what manner she'd style her hair or which of the young men she wanted to marry.

"May I have this next dance, miss?" The handsome man's blue eyes gleamed.

Carina glanced down, pretending to be shy but inwardly delighted. "Of course you may." She put her hand in his big, capable one then waltzed around the room. No worries, only her and the man, so tall. . .so comely. A suitor to win her affections?

No, not a suitor at all. The dancer turned into Johan. Sweet, gentle Johan.

The music suddenly changed. The soft harmonies fled as a harsh clanging bullied them away.

Bang! Bang!

Loud horns replaced the lyrical flute. Drums drowned out the violin.

No, not drums.

Pistols.

The stench of gunpowder instead of the sweet scent of flowers.

Blood. Johan's blood.

Her brother fell, his lifeblood draining from the wound in his belly. Carina screamed.

"Miz C'rina, wake up. I done knocked on yo' door, but you didn't answer. You's having another one of them dreams."

A hand jiggled her shoulder, and Carina opened her eyes. Her room took shape as she blinked away the sleepiness weighing down her eyelids. Sweat dampened her shirtwaist, her hair, and the right side of her face where it had lain against her hand. Her head ached, and her eyes felt as if she'd washed them out with salt water.

Etta stood over her, concern etching the girl's black eyes. Her frizzy hair refused to stay hidden under her red scarf, instead sticking out everywhere, giving her a whimsical look that fit her flighty personality.

Carina's heart still pounded from reliving that horrid day. Sunlight from the west flooded her room, reminding her it was afternoon, not morning. She had no cause to be in bed this time of day, and realizing that Etta of all people had found her so, irritated her. "Is something wrong?"

"Oh! Silly me. I done forgot." Etta straightened and lifted her fingers to her mouth. "Daddy said Abel hurt his leg out in the fields. He done sent Enoch over to the neighbors to see if'n Thomas can come and doctah him."

Carina's heart jolted. She couldn't lose a worker now that she'd leased out so many. "How bad is it?"

Etta shrugged and spun around, holding out her skirts and studying her reflection in the mirror. She swung back and forth, as if dancing.

"Etta!"

"Oh, uh. . .bad, I s'pose. Enoch, he was ridin' Comet."

It must be serious if Woodson allowed Enoch to take their fastest horse. Carina slid off the side of the bed, glanced at her own reflection, and winced. A large red circle resided where her hand had pressed against her cheek. Her hair wasn't much better than Etta's, but what did it matter? No one would see her except her people. "Go find your mama and tell her I said to bring the basket of medicines and bandages to the quarters."

"Yes'm." Etta yawned and strolled out of the room as if she hadn't a care in the world.

"Hurry!"

Etta jumped at Carina's loud bark and scurried down the hall and around the corner. Carina glanced down at her wrinkled skirt then fled the stuffy room. She could worry about her clothing later. Right now, she had to make sure Abel was all right. If anything happened to the jolly old man, she didn't know what she'd do. He was about the only person who could tug a smile from her solemn face.

As she passed by her fader's room, she slowed her steps and peeked in. The drapes were drawn, per his request, leaving the room hot and dusky. How could he stand it?

She tiptoed past the open door, glad that he was resting quietly. The way her emotions were today, she didn't know if she could endure another tongue-lashing from him, and once he learned the drastic step she'd taken today, one was sure to be coming. Maybe she just wouldn't tell him.

ஃ

Reed stood on the piazza overlooking the Reed Springs gardens. Scotland had been an experience he wouldn't have traded for anything, but it wasn't home, and nothing could compare to walking the halls of a home that had been in his family for generations. The garden had changed little in the three-odd years he'd been gone. Still perfectly manicured, like a beautiful woman dressed in her finery on her way to a ball. An artist's canvas of colors spread out before him—the vivid green of the grass and the palmettos lining the path to the dock; the blue of the Ashley River reflecting the sky; and the purples, yellows, and pinks of his mother's favorite flowers and shrubs. He'd be hard-pressed to explain to anyone how good it felt to be home again.

A knock sounded at his bedroom door; then it opened and his mother peeked in. "I heard you walking about. Are you decent yet?"

He chuckled. He'd been *decent* for more than two years now, ever since he met his Savior and dedicated his life to serving God. "Yes, Mother. Come on in."

Susan Bishop glided into his room, not looking a day older than when he'd left America. Though forty-four, she was still lovely. Her pecan-colored hair had yielded to gray along her hairline, but her face still had a rosy glow. Her brown eyes sparkled, revealing her delight at having him home again. She paused and glanced behind her, motioning to someone.

Penny, a new servant he'd met when he returned home yesterday, shuffled through the door, carrying a tray laden with breakfast foods. Reed hurried over to the table where he'd deposited his doctor's bag last evening and moved it to his bed. The tray clunked as Penny set it down.

"We didn't wait breakfast, since I knew you'd be exhausted from your travels and would most likely sleep late." His mother turned to the servant. "Thank you, Penny, you may go."

Penny curtsied then scurried from the room.

"I wasn't sure if you still drank coffee or if you've reverted back to the ways of your English ancestors and now drink mostly tea."

"Either one is fine, Mother."

She swatted her hand through the air. "I declare, what is this *Mother* bit? I've missed being called *Mama* for the past few years."

Reed lifted up one of the silver domes, revealing a bowl of porridge with a circle of melted yellow butter forming a pool in the center. He set the lid back down and peeked at another hidden delight. Two thick slices of ham lay nestled beside an omelet. His mouth watered. "You don't know how much I missed our fine Southern food, Mother."

Her thin brows lifted. "Mother?"

Reed shrugged and grinned. "Don't you think *Mama* is a bit childish for a man of twenty-three?"

She hiked her chin and straightened to her full five-foot-four height. "I do not, at least when we are home." She pulled out a chair. "Sit. Eat."

"Yes, Mama." He chuckled. "But only if you'll join me."

She nodded, her delight evident in her soft smile. She poured them both a cup of coffee, adding milk and sugar to hers.

Reed didn't know where to start first. A trio of tempting pastries formed a triangle on one plate, but it was the lure of the ham that pulled him the strongest. When was the last time he'd eaten meat and been certain what creature it came from? He loved Scotland and the Scots, but they sure ate some disgusting things.

"What was that shudder for? Is something not to your liking?" She reached to take away his plate of ham and eggs.

He grabbed it and lifted it out of her reach, grinning playfully at her. "Ah-ah. I'm not done with that yet, Mama." When she placed her hands back in her lap, he put his plate back on the table. "That shudder was because I was remembering some of the 'delicacies' we were encouraged to eat in Scotland."

His mother's eyebrows lifted. "Such as?"

"The worst of the lot was haggis." He couldn't help shuddering again. The one and only time he ate it, he'd spent the rest of the evening outside, retching. "It's a nasty-tasting dish of sheep's innards cooked in a sheep's stomach, and usually served with neeps and tatties."

His mother's eyes widened. "It all sounds so foreign. Haggis? Neets and tatties?"

"Neeps." He paused for a sip of coffee, closing his eyes as he relished its strong flavor. "Mmm. . .delicious." He took another long sip then bit off a hunk of ham. "Actually, the neeps were tolerable. They're some kind of mashed yellow turnips, and *tatties* are simply potatoes."

"Oh, I don't suppose I thought much about the food you were eating. I was more concerned that you were working too hard at your studies and then later in that infirmary. I prayed so hard that you wouldn't catch some horrid disease."

Reed reached over and patted her hand. "You needn't have worried. The Lord took care of me, even before I served Him."

Her broad smile warmed his heart.

"I can't tell you how it thrills me to hear you talking about our Lord. For so long I worried that you might not turn out well—and look at you now." She pulled her hand out from under his and laid it on top, squeezing his. "Are you content with your decision to become a doctor?"

He nodded. "Yes. I have no regrets."

Reed winced the moment the words left his mouth. He did have a regret—one that still haunted his dreams on occasion.

"What's wrong?"

He hung his head, trying to put from his mind that terrible day—the day he killed a man.

"You're remembering that duel, aren't you?"

He nodded, not all that surprised at his mother's perception.

"That was a long time ago, son. Fretting over it won't change anything. God has forgiven you, and you need to forgive yourself."

Glancing up, he didn't try to hide the pain he felt. "Just how do I do that? I'm a doctor—dedicated to helping people—but I shot my neighbor."

"Have you never lost a patient to death?"

Reed clenched his jaw. "Of course I have. But it's not the same." He stood and strode out onto the piazza. Leaning on the railing, he hung his head. He'd lost more patients than he could count. Medicine was a science, not a cure-all.

"It's not that much different. You had no malicious desire to inflict harm when you shot Johan Zimmer, did you?"

He shook his head. "I only sought to restore honor to Father and our family name, which Zimmer slandered in public. I should have just walked away and refused to fight."

His mother blew out a heavy sigh. "I don't condone dueling, by any means, but to have refused when Johan challenged you would have affected your standing in our community. There are plenty who think dueling is a barbaric way to settle people's differences—me included—but there are many others who'd refuse to do business with Reed Shipping if you'd said no. Things are slowly changing, thankfully. There's talk of initiating legislation to abolish dueling."

"That's a good thing then."

Reed dreaded the day when he'd have to face the Zimmers. Apologizing hardly seemed the proper thing to do given that so much time had passed, and even mentioning the deed was likely to cause hurt. But wouldn't just seeing him have the same effect on the Zimmers? He'd wrestled over and over with the idea of not returning to Charleston—about traveling out West, where no one knew what he'd done, but how could he do that to his mother after she'd waited so long for his return? He'd just have to face the Zimmers when the time came. "Do we still have the same neighbors?"

"Yes." His mother nodded. "Your cousins Seth and Emily Madison still live at Madison Gardens, at least when they're not in Charleston so he can run Reed Shipping." She gasped and turned toward him, touching his sleeve. "Did I write to you that Emily is with child? Now that you're home, you can deliver her baby."

Reed pursed his lips and shook his head. Though he wondered about the Madisons—had even received two letters from Seth—his mother had failed to discern the real meaning of his question about their neighbors. "Don't you think that would be a little awkward? Considering that I've known both Seth and Emily most of my life."

"Oh, pshaw. You're a doctor, and I'm sure Em would be thrilled to have an educated man tend her instead of a midwife."

He wasn't so sure, but voicing his opinion wouldn't change his mother's.

"And I guess you want to know—the Zimmers still own Tanglewood, although there is much less of it than when Karl first bought it."

"Tanglewood?"

"Yes. Didn't I write and tell you that's what Carina finally named it?"

He searched his mind but knew she hadn't. The fact that the German family hadn't named their estate had been fodder at gatherings for as long as they'd lived here. "No."

His mother's chest rose and fell as she sighed. "It's a fitting name for the place now. With Karl bedridden and Jo—uh. . ." She glanced up with a worried gaze.

"It's all right. You can say his name."

"Well, Carina has had her hands full hanging on to the place. I bought some land from her even though we didn't really need it."

Carina. He'd always liked that name, but he'd rarely seen the girl it belonged to. Before the ship sank with Karl's whole harvest aboard, he'd ridden over a time or two with his father. The small, dark-haired girl shied away from visitors, but he'd watched her from the window while their fathers conducted business. She was always herding Johan around. He was only an inch or two shorter than her then, but there was no doubt who ran the roost. A little female chick. Pretty, if his memory served him well.

"I feel so sorry for her. She never does anything but work. Never attends the balls or social events around here or in Charleston. I don't believe the poor girl knows how to have fun. Bless her heart."

In spite of the heaviness of the topic, Reed smiled. He'd missed hearing his mother's smooth Southern accent after listening to the hard-to-understand Scottish burr for so long.

Quick steps thumped down the hallway, stopping at his door. He and his mother turned in unison.

"Miz Bishop, pardon me, but Enoch from the Zimmers' is

at the door. He say one of them's workers is hurt and can he fetch Thomas back to tend him?"

"Of course—"

"No! I'll go."

Reed's mother sucked in a breath and grabbed his arm. "See that Enoch has a drink if he's thirsty, Penny." When the maid had gone, his mother gave him a stern look.

"What?" He strode across the room and opened his bag, knowing already that everything was in order.

"You know that most of the Reeds before us and then us Bishops have never owned slaves, but the Zimmers do. I'm not prejudiced, but many people around here would think less of you for tending to an injured slave. Are you certain you want to walk down that path? It could end your career as a doctor before it even begins."

"I pledged to care for any hurting person, no matter the color of his skin." He snapped the bag shut and reached for his frock coat. He was far less concerned about what people thought about him than he was worried about encountering a member of the Zimmer family. But he couldn't allow a man to suffer because the situation was awkward for him.

His mother nodded and smiled. "I'm happy to hear you say that, son. But just remember, things change slowly in the South. People here are steeped in tradition."

"I know, Mama. Now, I must go."

"All right. I'll gather some things and have Charley drive me over. Maybe there's something I can do to help. I can at least keep Carina company. She cares so much about her slaves that she's bound to be upset."

Reed strode from the room, thinking it ironic that Carina cared for her *slaves*. If she cared so much, she'd set them free.

five

Abel's groans tore at Carina's heart long before she reached the slave quarters. She'd had the elderly man's house built closest to the barn, hoping to save him a few steps each day. Why had he been working in the fields? Woodson had been instructed to give Abel only simple jobs like repairing harnesses, grooming the horses, and feeding livestock. She wanted him to feel useful, but she didn't want him out sweating in the hot sun. As odd as the situation was, he'd become her mentor and a friend, and she didn't want to lose him.

Little Sammy leaned against the door frame, staring inside. Tears streamed down his dark cheeks, but he didn't utter a sound. When he saw her, he ran to her, burying his face in her skirts. Carina patted his back and hugged him; then she stooped down. "Your mama is bringing bandages. I'd like you to go see if she needs help. Then I have a special job for you, if you're up to it."

Torn bits of leaves clung here and there to his curly black hair, as if he'd shredded a handful and tossed them in the air over his head. She plucked out the larger ones.

Sammy swiped his eyes with the back of his hands and stared up at her with watery eyes. "I's a man. I can do anythin', Miz Zimmer." The thin seven-year-old stood straight like a soldier then leaned over and wiped his damp cheek on his shoulder.

Smiling, Carina hoped to put the boy at ease and make him feel useful while getting him out from under foot. "I need

39

someone who can wait out front and tell Enoch and Thomas where we are. Can you do that?"

"Yes'm." He smiled then darted past her, his thumping bare feet pounding across the dirt path.

Stopping outside Abel's house, Carina stood beside the open door, half afraid to peek in. What if the injury were serious? Would he die?

She nibbled on the knuckle of her index finger, wishing there was someone else who could handle this crisis, but she had long ago learned that if she didn't do the tending, it wouldn't get done. Lowering her hand and straightening her spine, she stepped inside. "How is he, Woodson?"

Betsey's husband glanced up and gave a brief shake of his head. Chester, the other field hand, stood at the end of the bed, shifting from foot to foot.

Soft moans rose up from the lone bed. Abel lay in the shadows, his hand holding tight to the edge of the mattress. His right leg was bent like a stick snapped in two so unnaturally at the midcalf, but as far as she could tell, the wound hadn't pierced his skin. She despised seeing him suffering and chastised herself for worrying earlier about losing another worker when her good friend lay writhing in pain. People would look down on her if they knew that some of her father's slaves were her best friends. It was because of them that she found the strength to go on each day.

"Ches'er, go fetch me two fresh boards 'bout a foot-and-half long, and git some bandages from Betsey." The low timbre of Woodson's deep voice kicked Chester into action.

He hurried past Woodson, nearly running into her. His eyes widened; then he ducked his head. "Pardon, Miz 'Rina."

"That's all right. I snuck in quiet-like. I already have Betsey gathering the bandages."

Chester's eyes shone with unshed tears, and his lower lip quivered. "It were my fault, Miz 'Rina. I done left a spade out in the field. We was ready to come in, and Abel said he'd fetch the spade." His shoulders drooped and he shook his head. "Ol' Abel, he done stepped in a hole we hain't filled in yet. His leg snapped like a fox's in a trap." He made claws with his fingers then clapped his hands together.

Carina shuddered at the vivid demonstration. "It's all right, Chester. I know Abel doesn't blame you, and neither do I. Accidents happen." She knew the man's fears stemmed from her father's past harsh treatment. He would have beaten Chester severely not just for causing another worker to be injured but simply because he'd left a tool out in the weather. She believed in treating the slaves with kindness and received their loyalty for it.

Woodson cleared his throat and scowled at the younger man. Chester cast another glance at Abel then hurried out to do Woodson's bidding.

"What can I do to help?"

"Ain't nothin' to be done till I get some supplies, unless you want to snitch some of yo' daddy's whiskey to ease Abel's pain."

Carina despised drinking, and her fader had strict rules about not letting slaves have whiskey. He just didn't want to share, but in this one thing, she agreed. Liquor weakened people to where they couldn't function or think straight. It emboldened them to do things they wouldn't normally do. But it would ease Abel's pain. Could she sneak a small amount for Abel's sake without her fader noticing?

"I can try." She hurried outside, feeling guilty that she was relieved to have a task to do so she wouldn't have to witness Abel's suffering any longer. Poor old man.

She cut through the barn and scanned the area to make

sure the horses were all right; then she lifted up her skirt and jogged toward the house. The door to the kitchen flew open and banged against the side of the building. Betsey hustled out the door onto the whistling walk and hurried toward her.

"How's Abel? He be dead?"

Carina smiled. Betsey always expected the worse. "No, but he's in a lot of pain. Woodson wants me to sneak some of Fader's whiskey for him."

Betsey's eyes widened. "That be dangerous, even fo' you."

She nodded. "I know. I'll be careful—and quiet. Where's Etta? I don't want her down at the cabins, blubbering and upsetting Abel."

"I know. She be in the kitchen peelin' taters for supper."

"All right. I'm heading in the house and will be back in a few minutes. I hope."

Betsey tightened her lips then turned toward the barn and shuffled away, as fast as her wide body could travel.

Carina wiped her feet on the faded carpet runner just inside the side door. The poor thing was as sad as the rest of the house. She remembered the day it arrived on a wagon her father had driven from Charleston. Her mama had been so excited and had done a little jig in the yard, looping arms with Carina and swinging her around. Those had been happy days.

But happy days rarely occurred anymore. She didn't have time for them—nor lollygagging and dreaming about the past.

She tiptoed up the stairs, trying to step lightly so as to not put her full weight on the steps and make them squeak. Pausing at the entrance to her fader's room, she exhaled a soft sigh to see he was still sleeping—and that he'd rolled over so his back would be to her. If not for Abel's dire need, she'd never attempt such a feat.

Walking on her toes, she crept across the room, following the lone sliver of sunlight that defied the thick drapes. It led almost directly to the round drum table that held a tray with a single bottle and glass. Glancing sideways, she held her breath as she reached for the bottle.

Her fader snorted then rolled onto his back and scratched his chest through his nightshirt. Carina froze. All except for her trembling hand.

"Hey there, girl. What's that you're doing?"

৯

The warm breeze brushing Reed's cheeks as his horse galloped down the road confirmed that he was truly home. No more chilly days and frigid nights trying to keep warm in a drafty room. No more twenty-hour days working in a smelly infirmary filled with the sick and dying. No more odd Scottish food.

He much preferred helping people one-on-one—and tasty Southern cuisine.

As his horse approached the turnoff to Tanglewood, Reed slowed his mount to a trot. If he hadn't known where the entrance to the plantation was, he would have missed it. The quarter-mile drive was overgrown with trees with dead and broken limbs, shrubs that looked as if they were fighting one another to see which could get to the far side of the road first, and vines that battled the shrubs. An abundance of weeds with colorful flowers rose up between the wheel tracks in their effort to erase all evidence of human life.

Karl Zimmer must be terribly ill to allow his home to remain in such a state of disrepair. A shaft of guilt stabbed Reed. If he hadn't killed Johan in that duel, would Tanglewood be in such a dilapidated condition?

He nudged his mount into a gallop again. No amount of remorse could bring back the young man, and Reed had poured out enough remorse over the past few years to fill an ocean. He was a different man from that arrogant youth he'd once been. God had changed him, and now God was giving him a chance to help the Zimmers.

A young boy sat on the steps to the main entrance of the house. He jumped up and waved at Reed, his arms flapping like a bird not yet old enough to fly. Guiding his horse over to the child, he scanned the house and yard. It was in the same condition as the drive. Chipped paint curled up on the side of the house, like a beggar woman's tattered skirt, revealing a dingy gray petticoat.

"You come to he'p Abel? They's over at his cabin." The boy jumped off the top step and loped toward the barn.

Reed reined his horse to the left and followed. Instead of going into the faded barn, the boy skirted around it, sliding to a halt outside a small cabin.

"In there." The boy's thin finger disappeared behind the doorjamb.

Reed dismounted and held out the reins. "You think you could walk my horse and then get him a drink?"

A wide grin tugged at the boy's cheeks. Reed couldn't help noticing the child's spiked lashes. Had he been upset over the injured man or something else?

He untied his medical bag from the back of his saddle then ducked through the doorway. His eyes adjusted to the dimmer light as a moan rose up from across the small room. A tall, broad-shouldered man turned away from the bed and stared at Reed, as did a shorter and much wider woman. Neither said a word but stared at him as if he were an apparition. A dark stain covered the white of the man's shirt.

"I'm Dr. Reed Bishop. Can you tell me what's wrong with this man?"

The couple eyed one another. The woman's brows lifted, but the man gave a quick shake of his head. They kept their heads down as was the way of most slaves, but the tall man cleared his throat. "I reckon you be lookin' for Massa Zimmer. He up at the big house."

Karl Zimmer had been bedridden for a while—that was common knowledge. "Has he taken a turn for the worse?"

"Nah, sir. He be the same."

"Then I'll see to this man first. What's his name?"

The man's head jerked up, his eyes wide. "We ain't never had no real doctah tend any of us."

The woman's dark eyes brimmed with hope. "He be Abel, and his leg be broke."

The tall man shushed her and scowled. "Miz Zimmer, she done sent for someone already."

Reed heaved a sigh. He knew discrimination ran both directions at times, but would they stand in the way of his helping their friend just because he was white? "I know. Enoch came to my home—Reed Springs. I've just returned from Scotland, where I was educated at the Royal College of Physicians and Surgeons of Glasgow. I'm quite capable of tending your friend."

"Let the doctah be." A weak voice rose up from the bed, and the tall man turned and glanced down.

Reed got his first look at his patient—an older man. He was within his right to step forward and start assessing the injured party, but he waited. For some reason, he wanted the tall man's approval. Finally, Woodson nodded and stepped back.

Stooping down, Reed lifted Abel's wrist and checked his pulse. Weak but steady. He scanned the slave's length, narrowing in on the ripped pants and crooked leg. At least as best he could tell in the dim lighting, the broken bone wasn't protruding through the skin. *Thank You, Lord, for that.* "I need more light. Do you have a lantern?"

Woodson shook his head. "Massa Zimmer, he don't allow no fires near the barn."

Reed pursed his lips. He didn't like the idea of moving Abel, but he had to see well if he was going to help him. He held his bag out to the woman, who took it with lifted brows. "Woodson, I need you to lift that end of the mattress while I hoist this end. We'll take Abel outside where I have proper lighting."

Woodson hesitated.

"Go on, git hold of the bed." The old man swiped his hand in the air; then it dropped back to his side.

In less than a minute, they had Abel situated outside under the shade of an apple tree. The old man groaned but never cried out. Reed hated that moving his patient caused him additional pain, but it was necessary. He quickly assessed the man's injuries—a severely fractured leg, but that seemed the extent of it. Standing, Reed motioned to the two servants to come to him. "I need a bucket of water," he said to Woodson.

Nodding, Woodson jogged away. Reed turned to the woman. "Do you have any paperboard and some starch?"

Betsey's eyes rolled upward as she considered his question. Then she nodded so hard her jowls jiggled. "Yes, suh. I know just where some be." She turned and cupped her mouth with her hands. "Sammyyy! C'mere, boy."

A short while later, once all the supplies had been gathered, Reed dispensed a dose of laudanum and sent more prayers heavenward, asking God to help Abel endure setting the leg and the splinting procedure. Finally, he stood and surveyed his handiwork. Not too bad at all.

Betsey wiped Abel's brow with a damp cloth and cooed to

him. "You be all right soon enough. Mm-huh, you will."

Reed washed the starch mixture off his hands in the bucket of fresh water that Woodson had brought him then dried his hands with a clean towel. He offered Woodson and Betsey a smile. "With good fortune and God's healing hand, Abel should recover use of his leg, as long as he stays off of it for the next month, giving it time to heal well. Take special care that he not move his leg until the starch mixture hardens. Could take the rest of the day. You can give him a dose of laudanum for the pain." Reed showed Betsey how much to dispense. "But be careful that you don't give him too much. Mix it in a cup of willow-bark tea if he finds it too distasteful." At the sound of quick footsteps, he turned, flinging the towel over his shoulder.

The young boy, Sammy, who'd been tending his horse, ran toward him. He skidded to a halt, his eyes wide when his gaze dropped to the splint on the old man's leg. "How come Abel's leg done turned all white?"

"That be a splint," Betsey said. "It'll make Abel's leg better."

"How?"

Betsey shrugged. "Ask the doctah."

The boy spun toward Reed, but his eyes shot past him, just as Reed heard the soft swish of fabric. His heart jolted. A woman jogged toward him—a thin woman with enough curves to spark his interest, dressed in a faded brown skirt and off-white shirtwaist. He lifted his gaze to her face, and something hit him hard in the gut. Dark hair shoved up in a haphazard bun tilted to one side, and enticing wisps curled around her lightly tanned cheeks that would be an embarrassment to most Southern women. Eyes as mysterious as the ebony sky on a starless night stared down at Abel while her brow puckered to a V. Why was she so familiar?

Her gaze jerked up to Reed's and her enticing eyes went wide. She blinked several times, then her face scrunched like a grape left too long in the sun. "What are *you* doing here?"

A grin tugged at Reed's mouth. So much for Southern hospitality. That was hardly the thank-you he'd expected for risking his reputation to help her slave—at least he assumed Abel belonged to this intriguing woman.

That sense of knowing her—of seeing her before— flickered in his mind then exploded like a flame to whale oil. She was the black-eyed Susan from the ball—the same ball where he'd dueled Johan Zimmer. "And just who are *you*?"

She pursed her lips up to one side, then whisked around him as if he were of no more consequence than an old fence post. She stooped next to the old man. "How are you doing?"

The boy bounced on his toes and tugged on the woman's faded skirt. "Miz Zimmer, that doctah done put a cocoon on Abel's leg."

Zimmer? His vixen was Carina Zimmer? How could he have not known? He stepped back, staggering under the weight of this revelation. No wonder she'd refused to dance with him all those years ago at the ball.

She straightened and then marched toward him, her eyes slatted. "Who authorized you to treat my worker?"

Reed opened his mouth, but her reaction stunned him to silence. Any other Southern woman would graciously thank him for treating her slave, although she may well turn her back afterward and rant about how disgraceful a thing she thought it was. But not this woman. She didn't give a hoot about tradition but faced him head-on—and in spite of her rudeness, he couldn't help admiring her candor.

"I did not give you permission to be on my property, nor did I authorize you to treat one of my people. I want you to leave." She stamped her foot. "Now!"

Betsey hurried around behind Miss Zimmer, shoving Reed's instruments into his bag. He winced at the harsh treatment of the brand-new utensils that he hadn't had a chance to properly clean yet. The slave woman waddled over and held out his bag to him, the gratitude in her eyes palpable. He offered her a gentle smile and nodded his understanding, but the grin soon withered in the face of Miss Zimmer's anger.

"Well, are you leaving?"

"Miz Zimmer," Betsey said. "He done he'ped Abel out. He say that thing on Abel's leg will he'p it to heal better and make it stronger. Can't I at least offer him some pie and tea?"

Miss Zimmer scorched her maid with a glare then turned her incendiary gaze back on him. He should go. Although he hated to leave his patient so soon, he'd done all he needed to do for now. "Make sure Abel stays in bed for the next few weeks, and give him that dose of laudanum like I explained earlier. No walking or standing until I give permission. Woodson, let's get Abel back inside where he'll be more comfortable."

"We don't need help from a *Bishop*." Miss Zimmer nudged her chin toward the trail, her meaning evident.

Reed strode forward, stopping a few feet in front of her, and met her eye for eye. She had to tilt back her head to keep her glare locked onto his. He'd never noticed before the extraordinary length of her ebony lashes or that her eyes were so black the pupil and iris all but melded together. A strip of paler skin at the base of her neck moved as she swallowed hard—the only indication that he had any effect on her. He longed to slide his finger across her skin and see if it was as soft as he expected. He stepped back, and swallowed, too.

"I'll. . .uh. . .be back tomorrow—to check on my patient." He nodded to Woodson and Betsey then marched around Miss Zimmer and strode past the barn. Now where had that boy put his horse?

"Don't come back, Bishop." Miss Zimmer's harsh words snapped at his heels like a pesky terrier. "We Zimmers tend our own."

six

Reed marched back to the front of the barn, searched for his horse, and found him roped to a post near the water trough. Emotions battered him from all sides, like a rudderless ship tossed about on stormy waters. Anger swelled, but as it receded, guilt gnawed at him. Carina Zimmer had a right to be angry at him for all the pain he'd caused, but that didn't mean she could deny her servants proper medical treatment, especially when there were precious few surgeons willing to treat slaves.

He tossed the blanket onto the horse's back then set the saddle down and cinched it. His mother had ordered the saddle specially made with leather straps to hold his medical bag, but Reed didn't bother attaching it. Mounting in one swift movement, he just wanted to get away before he stormed back and said something to that irritating woman that he might regret.

The trail that led back to the road didn't just look shabby now. Instead it sent a message: stay away. Ride on past, and don't stop here. You're not welcome.

He drew in a breath through his nose and exhaled. What kind of life had Miss Zimmer lived that would make her so closed off and bitter? He thought of the differences in the two neighboring estates. Reed Springs was probably five times larger and kept in immaculate condition. His estate radiated life, prosperity, and openness, while Tanglewood represented failure, struggles, and death.

A motion in front of him caught his eye. A buggy turned

the corner and approached, carrying his mother, and behind it rode the Zimmers' man, Enoch. Miss Zimmer was in no mood for visiting, and he wasn't about to let that snippety woman lambast his well-meaning, kindhearted mother.

The buggy slowed and stopped. Reed didn't recognize the driver—a young man of about thirteen—but there was something familiar about him. Hadn't his mother said the boy's name was Charley?

His mother tilted back her head and peered out from under the brim of her bonnet. A wide blue ribbon, the color of the sea, wrapped around the hat and was tied in a huge bow beneath her chin. His mother always did love her bonnets. She smiled, and he remembered all the lonely nights in Scotland when he'd longed to see her face again. Nobody except for his heavenly Father loved him like his mother. "Are you finished already, son? The injury must not have been as bad as Enoch indicated."

"The man's leg was fractured. I splinted it."

His mother lifted her gloved fingertips to her lips. "Oh, the poor dear. When you come back to check on the man, you can bring Carina some of my willow-bark tea. That will ease the pain some."

"Miss Zimmer isn't receptive to receiving help from us Bishops. It's best you just turn around and head back home, Mother."

She pinched her lips as if tasting something sour then shook her head. "No, Carina is just upset at seeing you again after what you did, but she'll let me help her."

Reed stiffened. "After what *I* did?"

His mother glanced at the youth beside her. "You know."

Leaning forward, he met her gaze. "That was all Johan's doing. I had no intention of shooting him."

The boy's eyes widened, and he glanced at Reed's midsection, as if looking for a weapon.

"But you did, and it cost Carina her brother. Surely you can understand how seeing you again is upsetting her. She just needs time."

He raised his hands in surrender. "You should have stopped me from coming over if you knew that to be the case."

A gentle smile lifted her lips. "There's no stopping you when you've made up your mind."

≈

Reed stood on the piazza and watched a rabbit hopping from one spot in the lustrous grass to another. It paused, lifted up its head, and looked around, then dipped its head and came up chewing. It hopped to another spot and did the dance all over again. Such a serene scene.

A yawn slipped out. He leaned his weight against the railing and looked to the east, where the Zimmer plantation resided two miles away. Had Abel slept any better than Reed? Was that stubborn Miss Zimmer up yet? It was common knowledge that many Southern belles stayed up late at night when the temperatures were cooler then slept late into the morning, but he couldn't imagine Carina Zimmer enjoying such luxuries.

He sipped his lukewarm tea, trying to decide whether to ride over to Tanglewood or not. The doctor in him felt the need to check on his patient, but he also ought to honor Miss Zimmer's request to stay off her land.

Long lashes and fiery eyes had invaded his dreams the night before. He heard her screams over and over as her brother fell to the ground, bleeding. He saw the blood on the man's shirt as he all but ran from the scene. Rubbing his arm where Johan's shot had grazed it, he relived that horrible day.

He hadn't wanted to shoot but had reacted and accidentally pulled the trigger. Intentional or not, the result was the same. A young man had died at his hand.

A knock sounded on his bedroom door. He turned and padded into the room, noticing a young Negro servant waiting in the hall. Her yellow dress reminded him of the one that Miss Zimmer had worn at the ball, except the fabric of this dress was stiff with newness and vivid in color. Why would such a thing sadden him?

He lifted his brows. "Yes? Tansy, isn't it?"

The young woman nodded but kept her head down, revealing the floral pattern of her multicolored head scarf. "Miz Bishop wants to know if'n you is gonna eat breakfast downstairs with her or in yo' room."

"Tell her I'll be right down."

Tansy gave a quick shake of her head, a brief curtsy, and scurried away. Reed grinned. His being home had set on edge the newer staff, although those servants who had been around most of his life seemed delighted to have him home again.

He dropped into a rococo side chair, pulled on his boots, then jogged down the stairs. His mother was already seated, sipping her tea. Her gaze snapped to his as he crossed the room, and she smiled warmly. "Good morning, son."

She stared at him as if unable to tear her gaze away. "I'm still getting used to your being home. Sometimes I declare it must be a dream. I missed you so much." She blinked her eyes as if to stem tears.

"So did I." He cleared the tightness from his throat, pulled out the chair at the head of the table, and sat.

"You missed yourself?" She giggled and covered her mouth.

"What? Oh." Reed grinned. "No, Mama, I missed you."

She hid her smile with a sip of tea. Tiny lines crinkled in

the corner of her eyes. Sparse webs of gray spread from her temple back to where they disappeared among the darker strands of her hair, which had been plaited, curled, and pinned perfectly on the back of her head. His mother's hair lay flat against her head, and not a single strand dared to poke up its head for fear of being snipped off. Such a contrast to Miss Zimmer, whose hair reminded him of the fuzzy-haired Scottish sheep.

His mother tapped her fingernail against her saucer, making a tiny clinking sound. "What are your plans now that you've returned home?"

Reed stared into his teacup. He'd contemplated the same thing many times. Should he move to Charleston and set up a practice or remain on the plantation where he'd have less opportunity to tend the sick and injured but would be near his mother? "I honestly don't know."

"I'm sure you want to serve as a surgeon, but I'd love to see you take over the operations of the plantation. It is your inheritance, after all."

Reed pursed his lips. The plantation had always been the one bone of contention between his mother and him, ever since his father passed on. He loved his home, but becoming a planter had never been his dream. All his life he'd cared for injured animals. Training to be a surgeon had been the realization of his biggest dream. "Harley seems to have things under his control. Reed Springs has fared well these years I've been gone, hasn't it?"

She nodded, but it was obvious that his response didn't please her. "That's true, but Harley is just a hired man, not an actual owner."

Reed caught his mother's gaze. Her brown eyes conveyed the turmoil going on inside her. Why couldn't she understand his need to ease people's suffering and mend their wounds? Why must the plantation always come between them? "You asked what I intended to do, Mother." He broke her gaze, unable to see the hurt in hers, and stared out the open window. "I'd like to find a spot of land closer to the main road and build a clinic."

She sucked in a breath but didn't say anything.

Could she not see that even this was a compromise for him? If he lived in Charleston or another town, he'd see a number of patients daily. By living at Reed Springs, he'd be close to her and could share most meals, but he'd never have the patient traffic he would in a city.

Footsteps sounded in the entry, and the footman cleared his throat. The man held a silver tray with a missive on it in one hand. Reed's mother slowly turned her head as if it were an effort. Knowing he disappointed her weighted down Reed's shoulders as if he were carrying a hundred-pound sack of rice.

"What is it, Jarrod?"

"A letter has arrived for Mr. Bishop, ma'am."

Reed's gaze jerked to the silver tray. Had the invitations to balls already begun to arrive? He had dreaded attending one, ever since the duel.

"You may bring it to Reed."

The footman nodded and strode forward, stopping on Reed's left. He held out the tray, Reed took the sealed note, and the footman left the room. A scrolling Z had been pressed into the wax seal. He searched his mind, trying to think of a friend or acquaintance whose last name started with a Z, but nothing came to mind.

"Well, are you going to stare at that note all morning?"

Reed slid his index finger under the flap and popped the wax seal loose. The terse note chilled him as much as if he'd fallen in the river in midwinter.

"What does it say? Bad news, from the look on your face."
He scanned the message again. Surely he'd misread it:

I challenge Reed Bishop to a duel at dawn, two days hence, at the dock at Tanglewood.

Carina Zimmer

seven

Reed hunkered low as the wind and horse's mane whipped his face. The animal's hooves thundered down the dirt road toward Tanglewood. He had decided to abide by Miss Zimmer's wishes and stay off her land, but her ridiculous challenge had changed his mind. Had the woman no sense at all?

Who would care for her father or her plantation or her slaves if something happened to her? Did she honestly think she had a chance shooting against a man who was an expert shot?

Not that he liked shooting, but his father had taken pride in his natural ability. It never mattered to his father that it cut Reed to the quick to kill an animal they needed for food. The family had to survive, his father always said, and a man had to provide for his family. He was much relieved when Harley had suggested raising beef. Reed had always made sure to be in Charleston or away some other place when it was time for slaughtering. He didn't want to seem lily-livered, but he couldn't bear to witness such an event.

His mount galloped down the lane toward the Zimmer home. He'd say his piece to Miss Carina Zimmer, check on his patient, then leave this run-down joke of a plantation.

As he neared the house, he reined in his horse and dismounted while the gelding was still walking. He dropped the reins, knowing the animal wouldn't go far, and climbed the steps two at a time. Reed pounded on the front door so hard it hurt his fist. When no answer came, he rapped on it with his other hand, just a bit more gently.

The door finally jerked open, and Betsey stood there with wide eyes. "Great day in the morning!" She glanced over her shoulder then back at him. "What you doin' here, Doctah Boss?"

Reed's anger dimmed at her uncouth greeting. And Dr. Boss? Where had she come up with that nomenclature? He shook off any traces of humor and reminded himself of Miss Zimmer's challenge. "I need to see your mistress."

Betsey's head swiveled back and forth. "Huh-uh. No, you don't."

Reed lifted a brow, more than a little surprised that Betsey would correct a visitor. A smidgen of fear passed through the slave's eyes, sending instant regret coursing through him.

"Miss Zimmer, she don't want to see you, sir. You bein' a Bishop an' all."

"I can't help who I am. I need to speak with her."

Betsey pressed her lips together and peeked behind her again. The heavyset woman shifted from foot to foot, obviously uncertain as to what to do.

Reed decided to let her off the hook. "I'll go check on Abel. Maybe you could let Miss Zimmer know that I'm here and would like to talk to her."

She bobbed her head up and down, her relief evident. "I can do that, sir. Mmm-hmm, I can."

He spun around and crossed the yard, having no doubt that once Carina Zimmer learned he was there, she'd come to chase him away like a hound dog after a rat. He wished he hadn't run off in such a rush and had thought to grab his medical bag.

Reed halted at the open door of Abel's cabin. Knocking at a slave's door felt odd, but barging on in didn't sit right with him, either. He stood staring at the opening a moment then looked around for Woodson. At this hour, the man was most likely out in the fields. No one else was around, either. Reed sighed.

"C'mon on in, whoever is out there." Abel's faint voice drifted out the door.

Reed stepped inside. "How are you doing today?"

"Better'n yesterday." Abel chuckled then groaned.

Smiling, Reed crossed over to the man's bedside. He checked his pulse—strong enough—and felt the man's forehead. Thank the good Lord there was no fever. "How is the pain?"

"Well, it's there, but not so bad if'n I swallow that nasty med'cine."

Feeling more confident that the man would survive, Reed relaxed. He checked to make sure the splint had hardened as he'd hoped. "Just make sure that you stay off that leg. No standing or working for a while."

Abel pursed his lips. "I can sit and mend tack and stuff. Maybe make some nails."

Reed shook his head. "Not this week. I want you flat on your back. I'll check again in a few days, and if you're still doing well, we'll try sitting you up. You'll probably be dizzy as long as you're taking the laudanum, but you need it until the pain in your leg dulls."

Abel scowled.

"I'll talk with Miss Zimmer to make sure she understands why it's important that she not push you to work more than I say you can."

The old man's gaze shot to his. "Miz 'Rina, she won't hardly let me work the ways things were. A man's gotta work, Doctah Boss."

Reed tried not to smile at the second use of the odd nickname. One of the slaves must have referred to him by that name, and the others had picked up on it. He squatted down to be on Abel's level. "A man needs to be able to walk to do most chores. You can best serve Miss Zimmer by getting well, and if you want to walk again, you need to follow my instructions."

Abel worked his mouth as if to say something but simply nodded. He yawned and closed his eyes. Reed stood and tiptoed out of the warm cabin. The cooler breeze instantly refreshed him. He glanced down the row of ten slave cabins, noting that of all the buildings he'd seen so far at Tanglewood, surprisingly they were in the best condition. The wood had not yet faded completely, and though they were not as nice as the two-room cabins with lofts that the Reed Springs servants lived in, they were by far better than most slave quarters. Few that he'd seen on other plantations even had furniture. It would seem that Miss Zimmer took better care of her slaves than she did herself. In spite of her challenge to a duel, that thought elevated his opinion of her. He still didn't agree with owning slaves, but hers were healthy, well fed, and well cared for. Quite the dichotomy.

He strode back past the barn, where several slats had fallen loose and lay on the ground. The odor of manure and hay emanated from the building. He picked up a board and studied it. The plank was still of fair quality and could be reused if a man had a nail and hammer.

His horse grazed contentedly near the paddock, and since no one was about, Reed walked into the barn and looked around. This place was not neat and orderly as his barn was. Instead of the tools being hung up in a tack room, racks, shovels, and hay forks lay dumped together in a heap. A few bridles hung by nails on one wall, and just two saddles set on lopsided racks.

The compact gray horse stuck its pretty head over the stall gate and whickered to him. He crossed over to it and scratched its head. "Well. . .good morning."

The horse nudged his hand as if asking for more attention. He ran his gaze along its shoulder, back, and rump. Other than being on the thin side and having its right front cannon wrapped, the animal looked fairly healthy.

"What are you doing to my horse?"

He spun around at the harsh feminine voice. Miss Zimmer stomped toward him, wearing the same outfit as yesterday—faded white blouse, worn skirt, and a scowl.

Reed raised his hands in surrender. "Just looking at her. She's a fine animal. An Arabian, I'm guessing. Though I've only seen a few of them."

Miss Zimmer's expression softened as her gaze shifted from him to her horse. Why should that bother him?

She shook her head and walked toward him. "No, Lulu is a Morgan."

His gaze swiveled back to the animal. Compact and sturdy with strong limbs, arched neck, and an expressive face. "I should have recognized her breed. My father had several Morgans back when he used to harness race. Though I don't ever remember seeing a gray one."

"They're not as common as bays, blacks, or chestnuts, but I think she's much prettier."

Reed caught Miss Zimmer's gaze, intrigued with her dark eyes. "Mmm. . .lovely."

She blinked, her cheeks grew crimson, then she scowled and stepped back. "Why are you here again? Our duel is tomorrow."

"No, it is not."

Her brow crinkled a moment; then her expression grew

serious. "Yes, it is."

Reed stepped closer. "No. It is not. I refuse to participate in another duel, especially one against a woman."

Her eyelids narrowed to a mere slit; her nostrils flared. The crimson on her face now wasn't from embarrassment. She spun away from him, flinging a light floral scent in his direction. Her hair, though unruly in its loose bun that threatened to unwind at any moment, looked clean and shiny. Her clothing was another thing—shabby, just like her property. Now that he thought about it, Betsey's dress was newer than her mistress's. He longed to take Miss Zimmer to Charleston—to see her dress like any other plantation mistress—but he'd have to hog-tie her to get her there. He closed his eyes and shook his head. How could he be attracted to this woman? She wanted him dead—and she wanted to be the one to pull the trigger.

"What's wrong? Are you ill?"

The unexpected compassion in her voice took him by surprise. He longed to make peace with her. "Yes, in a manner. I'm sick of this feud. Can't we set it aside and be friends? We are not our fathers. I'm sorry that your father lost his harvest and had financial troubles because our ship sank. But have you ever considered that we lost an expensive ship and a portion of our harvest, too?"

She blinked, a confused look crossing her face; then her gaze hardened. "But you didn't lose a brother."

He glanced down at the ground. "I never had one to lose, but my only sister died shortly after her birth."

Her mouth gaped open, but she wasn't ready to give up the fight. Her pert chin lifted. "I demand that you give me the satisfaction to right the wrong you did when you shot my brother. I expect you to be at the dock tomorrow at dawn. And no need to bring a second. We will deal with one another directly."

She spun around, not waiting for his response. Did she actually think he would duel with her? He marched after her.

"I'm not battling pistols with you."

Flinging out her arms, she pivoted as gracefully as a belle at a ball. "*Ja*, you will—or I'll come to your home and hunt you down."

He stared at her a long moment. Wishing things were different wouldn't change how they actually were. "I believe you would. But are you willing to shoot me in cold blood? Because I will not fire at you."

Her lips puckered and a myriad of expressions dashed across her pretty face. She tramped right up to him, stopping so close that if he as much as twitched he'd touch her. Tilting her head back, she glared up at him, nostrils flaring like a wild filly. The warmth of her breath feathered his face. If he leaned forward a few inches, he could steal a kiss. He almost smiled at the thought but worked hard to keep his expression somber.

"You Bishops are responsible for everything bad that has ever happened to us. I never even wanted to come to this country in the first place, but my fader had to have his way. My mother died as a result, now Fader is wasting away and doing nothing but sleeping and drinking, and Johan is lost to me. You'd be doing me a favor by shooting me, Mr. Bishop."

"Well, I won't. You can be sure of it. And I won't be at the dock tomorrow morn."

ಶ

Carina couldn't believe that Reed Bishop actually had showed up at the dock, after the adamant way he staunchly said he wouldn't. Her fader sure didn't think he had the nerve to face her in a duel, but this wasn't the first time he'd been wrong. The shimmering morning sun, peering over the horizon like a beacon lighting the way, silhouetted Mr. Bishop as he walked his horse along the banks of the Ashley River, in no apparent hurry to arrive at his destination. Part of her hoped that he wouldn't come. She hadn't been thinking clearly when she'd challenged him, but pride and stubbornness would not allow her to withdraw. What would happen to Tanglewood—to her people, her fader—if she was to perish in this duel? Of course, being a surgeon and a fine shot, Mr. Bishop could choose to wound her in a nonvital spot, then patch her up and go on his way, his satisfaction intact. But would she be satisfied?

No, that wouldn't do at all. She had too much work to do to be bedridden with a wound. She'd just have to shoot him first. Swallowing hard, she paced the damp grass, the hem of her skirts growing wetter by the second. Could she actually shoot him?

Wasn't that why she'd practiced over and over, all these years? Why she had become an expert shot? To extract vengeance on the man who had killed her brother? The man whose family had started her father's downhill spiral.

Betsey's warning—a verse from the Bible—rang clear in her mind, *Avenge not yourselves, but rather give place unto wrath: for it is written, Vengeance is mine; I will repay, saith the Lord.* She glanced down at the box of dueling pistols she'd borrowed from her fader's collection, uncertainty battling the desire for revenge.

She should never have told Betsey about the duel, but she had to let someone know—in case things went the wrong way. The woman had pitched a conniption fit, telling her what a fool she was for sending that written challenge and how good a man Doctah Boss was and how he'd helped Abel when no other white surgeon would have come near him with a ten-foot pole.

A chickadee called out a tune in the trees to the left, drawing her attention. She turned away from Mr. Bishop, who had dismounted and was walking her way. Was she wrong? All night she'd wrestled with her decision. Who else was there to stand up and demand satisfaction for the way her family had been wronged?

Forgive and forget, that's what Betsey said.

But for as long as she could remember, her fader had blamed Frank Bishop for his financial demise and later Reed Bishop for killing his only son and heir.

Carina's lip quivered. After all she'd done to keep the plantation going, her fader never once recognized her efforts or mentioned her as being his only heir. It was always her brother. What would happen when her fader died?

She huffed a harsh laugh. Maybe she would die today, and then maybe he'd bemoan her passing, but she doubted it. No matter how hard she worked, she could never gain his approval. Karl Zimmer had always been a demanding man, and being bedridden hadn't changed a thing. The only good she'd done was to help her slaves live a better life. At least they would be sad if she did not survive.

She had to see this thing through. If she lived, so be it, and if not, then her worries would be over. She spun around and marched toward Reed Bishop.

Like a pesky fly buzzing around her head, she heard Betsey's warning. "You ain't ready to die. You ain't made things right with the good Lord." She waved her hand in front of her face as if to drive away the taunting, but she just succeeded in gaining Mr. Bishop's attention. She lifted her chin. "I'm glad to see you actually showed up."

He removed his hat and held it in his hands. His brown hair, the color of one of Betsey's sweetgrass baskets, curled slightly in an enticing manner. Would it be soft to touch or stiff like Lulu's mane? His brow creased, but even so, he was still a handsome man. "Are you truly glad?"

The sad expression in his vivid blue eyes gave her pause, not to mention his unexpected question. Did it bother him to think she wanted him dead? And did she really? "I. . .uh. . .of course. One can't participate in a duel by oneself."

He sniffed a laugh and gave her a tight-lipped smile of resignation. She hadn't expected him to be sad. Did he truly think he would perish today?

She stiffened her back, opened the box of pistols, and held it out to him. "Choose your weapon, sir."

His eyes lifted to hers. "You actually mean to follow through with this ridiculous contest?"

Tilting her head back, she gazed into his eyes. If she killed him, she'd never again see those beautiful eyes. And his mother—the only neighbor who had reached out to her—would be heartbroken and never forgive her. It pained her to think of Susan grieving for her son. Until this moment, she had only thought that killing Reed Bishop would take away the pain of Johan's loss, but two wrongs didn't make a right. She would have to be satisfied with just wounding him. She grimaced but nodded. "I do. You took my beloved brother from me, not to mention our family's fortune."

He slapped his hat back on his head and shoved his hands to his hips. He cut a fine figure in his tan frock coat, gold brocade waistcoat, and dark-brown trousers tucked into his boots. "I've already explained about what happened between our fathers. Losing a shipment to weather or thieves is an unfortunate incident that too often occurs when merchants do business. As for your brother, he challenged me. It wasn't the other way around."

"Johan was a quiet, gentle soul. He never fought anyone and preferred gaining book knowledge to physical pursuits." She blinked and stepped back, feeling as if she couldn't breathe. She'd heard rumors whispered about that Johan had been the one to issue the challenge to duel, but she'd never believed it. And she didn't believe it now. "That's impossible. Johan would never do such a thing."

"Ha!" Mr. Bishop tossed his hands out to his side. "You were there. Did you not hear him? Your brother was drunk, Miss Zimmer. The liquor in his system must have emboldened him."

Several thoughts dashed across her mind. Her father complaining that some of his liquor was missing just before the duel. Of smelling the foul stench on Johan that day he'd been shot. Was it possible he'd drunk himself into a stupor that empowered him to do something so completely out of character? She shook her head. "No, I don't believe you."

He hung his head as if disappointed in her and kicked a stone, sending it spiraling toward the riverbank. Why should that bother her? He heaved a loud sigh and looked up, his gaze pleading. "I was leaving the day after that ball. I was on my way to become a surgeon—a man who heals people. Why would I challenge a man to a duel that might end his life? I'm a man of healing, Miss Zimmer, not hurting."

"But you hurt my brother. You *killed* him."

"I never meant to. I wasn't even going to fire at him, but when his lead ball hit my arm, I jumped and my finger pulled the trigger by accident."

"Ha!" Carina barked a laugh. "You expect me to believe that the shot that killed my brother was an accident?"

He nodded. "Yes, because it was."

Reed Bishop looked so sincere she almost believed him. If she hadn't known without a doubt that Johan could never do such a thing, she might have been swayed. But the truth was Reed Bishop had killed the only family member who loved her. She'd been less than two when their mother had died giving birth to Johan. For as long as she could remember, she'd helped take care of him. And now he was gone.

She lifted the pistols again. "Choose your weapon, and do it now."

Mr. Bishop stared at her, a muscle twitching in his clean-shaven jaw. His gaze dropped to the guns, and after a long moment, he selected one. He loaded the weapon then waited while she set down the box and finished loading hers.

"I have one favor to ask, Miss Zimmer."

Carina's heart jumped. What could he possibly want from her? "What's that?"

The muscles in his jaw flexed, and he blew a long breath from his nose. He caught her gaze, sending her stomach into spasms.

"If I perish, promise me that you'll see to it that my mother is well cared for. I don't want her to suffer because she has no one special in her life who loves her like I do."

She narrowed her eyes. Was this merely a ploy for her sympathy? Did he not know that she had lived the last four years grieving, angry, and plotting revenge as his mother would if he died today? Yet thinking of Susan Bishop having to endure such agony made her stomach ache. Watching over his mother was the least she could do, not that his mother would want to have anything to do with her after the duel if her son died at her hand. She nodded. "I promise. Now, walk ten paces then turn and fire."

He stared at her, nothing moving but his lashes and a muscle in his jaw. "As you wish, Miss Zimmer. Take your best shot, and I hope and pray that it relieves you of the terrible burden you're carrying."

eight

Stubborn, mulish woman—beautiful woman.

Did she honestly believe he could shoot her?

She didn't know him very well if she believed that.

In truth, she barely knew him at all.

He counted to ten in his head as he walked back toward his horse. He hadn't thought Miss Zimmer would actually go through with the duel, or he would have left the roan in a better place where he couldn't accidentally catch a lead ball fired by an incompetent shooter. He had no real fear that Miss Zimmer would actually hit him, yet knowing that he'd never intended to shoot Johan either left him a bit uneasy.

He wouldn't shoot her, no matter what. He couldn't live with himself if he damaged her lovely flesh or caused her pain. But he *had* inflicted pain—the deep, grieving pain of loss. He knew how it felt because he still missed his father, even though they were often at odds with one another.

He reached number ten in his count and turned. Carina Zimmer had already turned and pointed her pistol at him. Never once in the times he'd relived that duel with her brother had he ever dreamed he'd find himself in such a predicament. He caught her gaze and fired his pistol into the air, knowing that doing so violated code duello's rules for proper dueling. But there was hardly anything proper in a pistol battle with a woman.

Her mouth dropped open then snapped shut. She turned slightly sideways and aimed her pistol at him like a professional shootist might. A bead of sweat ran down his cheek as he lowered his weapon to his side. He had assumed Miss Zimmer didn't know how to shoot—a bad assumption on his part if her stance was any indication. Standing firm, he met her gaze for gaze. She held steady but didn't fire. *Father, watch over me. Keep Mother in the shelter of Your arms should I perish today.*

His opponent's pistol lowered, but she jerked it back up.

It wobbled.

She steadied it again and took aim. His heart pounded a frantic beat like it had the first time he performed a surgery. He took a deep breath and turned sideways as she had, making himself a smaller target. He didn't plan on making things any easier for her. His medical bag was on his horse, so if she didn't inflict too serious a wound, he might be able to treat himself.

Suddenly her pistol shimmied and fell to her side. She dropped it and hunched over, crying out a sob that went clear to his soul. He wasn't sure whether to shout a hallelujah, hurry to his horse and hightail it home, or wait. He doubted Miss Zimmer would be happy that he'd witnessed her collapse.

He took a step toward her. He couldn't just walk away and leave her all alone in her misery. Besides, she might get a sudden urge of boldness and shoot him in the back. He took another step and then another. Her soft sobs tore at his gut. *Comfort her, Lord.*

The next instant, he felt as if God had told *him* to comfort her. He stopped in front of her, but she seemed not to see him. He lifted his arms, stepped forward, and wrapped them around her. She stiffened for a moment then fell against his chest, crying more than he'd ever witnessed a woman cry.

"You're all right. Don't fret," Reed cooed to her. He

muttered prayers heavenward and patted her back. He longed to help her, to make her life easier, if only she'd let him. But he was probably the last person she'd accept assistance from. *Show me what to do, Lord.*

She clutched his shirt and leaned into his chest. His heart ached for her. She had so much responsibility on her slight shoulders. He thought of his mother and how she had run the plantation for so many years, all on her own. How was she able to keep things running so smoothly, but Miss Zimmer wasn't? He had it within his power now to make life easier for his mother. Guilt gnawed at him like a rat in a bag of grain.

Reed longed to lean his cheek against the top of Carina's head, but he resisted. He might be unable to deny a growing desire to know her better, but he didn't harbor any false hopes that she felt the same. Was she even aware that he held her in his arms?

ॐ

Carina stiffened. What was she doing enfolded in Reed Bishop's arms?

She couldn't shoot him, especially after he discharged his pistol in the air and stood still, waiting for her shot. How could he be so gallant in the face of death? How could the arms of her mortal enemy feel so safe? So good? So comforting?

When was the last time someone other than Betsey had hugged her? Reassured her? And why was he doing so when she'd come within a hair's length of shooting him?

He was still her nemesis. And she had a death grip on his waistcoat.

She released it suddenly and stepped back. His arms loosened but didn't let her go, as if he enjoyed holding her. She kept her gaze on the ground, too embarrassed to look up. "Please, let me go."

"I'd prefer not to."

Her gaze lifted to his of its own accord, and the tenderness in his eyes took her breath away. Was he merely attempting to use kindness to get her to forget about the duel? Their feud?

She stiffened her back and hiked her chin. "Turn loose of me, Mr. Bishop."

He heaved a sigh that washed across her face and dropped his arms so fast that she wobbled and had to grasp his arm to steady herself. Now that she was adrift from him, the loneliness rushed back. How could she betray her family by taking comfort from her enemy? Why did he of all people have to be her one adversary?

She turned her back to him and wiped her face with her sleeve. How could she ever face him again?

She couldn't.

Carina bent, picked up her pistol, and discharged it toward the river. Mr. Bishop jumped at the loud blast. He must have thought she could actually go through with shooting him— and that saddened her. But what else should she expect after the way she'd treated him?

Making a wide arc, she passed by him and retrieved the pistol case and his weapon, which lay on the damp ground where he'd dropped it. She would clean the weapons later. Right now she merely wanted to collect them and make a quick retreat back home.

She felt his eyes on her, but she couldn't face him again. The way he'd stood there, patiently waiting for her to kill or maim him, had completely disarmed her. Had stolen her anger and hatred. She'd come to the river expecting to die or at least to be injured, but he had willingly become the scapegoat, and she didn't know how to handle that.

She'd been angry for so long that she didn't know what to

do, so she merely headed for home.

Maybe tomorrow when the duel wasn't so fresh in her mind, she'd round up her anger and feel normal again.

❧

Reed hated to see her go, looking so dejected and alone. He doubted he'd ever forget how good it felt to hold her in his arms. She wasn't the first woman he'd hugged, but with the exception of his mother, she was the only one since he'd given his heart to God. Holding the sobbing Miss Zimmer had filled an empty place in him that those teasing, painted women from the taverns he used to frequent never could.

He felt as if she'd taken a part of him with her, and he wouldn't be whole again until he was with her. He released a loud sigh.

What in the world was wrong with him? He was pining for a woman who hated him—a woman who'd nearly sent him to his Maker.

He shook his head and strode toward his horse. He mounted but had no desire to move on. How did one go from expecting to be dead to living out the rest of the day as if nothing had happened?

His horse nibbled at the ankle-high grass and meandered just so that if Reed lifted his head, he could see Miss Zimmer hightailing it back home. What was she thinking? Had this duel settled anything?

"Please, Lord, make it so. Relieve Miss Zimmer of the heavy burden that she's carrying. Help her to forgive me."

He sat praying and enjoying the serene setting. Water swished softly through the tall marsh grass, and a trio of turtles sunned themselves on a large, flat rock near the bank. Yellow butterflies flittered from one wildflower to another. Cypress trees with their knobby roots, flowering dogwoods, and mossy oaks lined the edges of the river. This was a place so filled with life.

Reed heaved another sigh and reined his mount toward home. Now that he was going to live another day or so, he needed to hire someone to build his office. He'd ask Harley, since it was a sore spot with his mother.

He reined the roan to a halt just outside the barn and dismounted. The same young man who'd driven his mother to Tanglewood hurried out to receive the horse.

Reed unfastened his medical bag and nodded his thanks to the youth. "Make sure to brush him down and give him some oats."

"Yes, sir, Mistah Reed. I always do. Caesar, he's a good horse."

Charley led the gelding into the barn, and Reed followed him. He walked from stall to stall, studying the horses. He was going to need one of his own since he'd be staying at the plantation, and though Caesar was a decent horse, Reed found his particular gait uncomfortable. He wasn't ready to relegate himself to a buggy that doctors so commonly drove. A good saddle horse would do him well. "Which of these is the best horse for riding long distances?"

Charley crinkled up his nose. "Well, sir, I don't rightly know, beings as how I ain't never rode one very far."

Reed pursed his lips. He should have thought about that. A Negro—free or slave—riding along on a fine horse was bound to be stopped and most likely harassed. If he didn't have the proper papers, he could be in trouble. "Which one does Harley ride most often?"

"That'd be Pete. He's the big dun that stays in that third stall over there." Charley pointed across the barn.

Reed thanked him and strode up to the house. The more

he thought about it, the more he liked the idea of buying a horse of his own. Maybe he could talk his mother into going to Charleston for a few days to shop while he searched for a good horse. He smacked his riding gloves against his palm, liking the idea more and more. That would also give him the opportunity to research and locate a carpenter to design and build his office.

As he passed through the gardens, his stomach growled, reminding him that he hadn't yet eaten breakfast. He left before Cook had anything prepared this morning, not that he had much appetite given the circumstances. Now he was starving and ready for just about anything Cook could dish up.

He had a lot to be thankful for. He was still alive, as was Miss Zimmer, and both unharmed. Maybe things today had put in motion the end of the troubles between his family and the Zimmers. He'd held Carina in his arms and knew one thing for certain: For some odd reason, he liked her. More than liked her. He was attracted to her like he'd never been to any other woman.

The big question, however, remained: What was he going to do about that?

nine

"Carina! Amos!"

At her fader's sudden cry, Carina tossed down her hairbrush and ran down the hall. What would he say when she told him that Amos was no longer here, and neither were five other of their slaves? She'd managed not to tell him by simply avoiding him and staying busy away from the house. But it was bedtime, and he knew she'd be home. There was no evading him this time.

She skidded to a halt on the wood floor just outside his bedroom door. Her hand lifted to her nose at the sour odor emanating from the room. "Ja, Fader, what is it you need?"

"Where's Amos? He missed giving me a bath yesterday. I got sick today and retched all over myself. The stench is unbearable. Where is that boy?"

"Didn't Betsey clean you up and give you a fresh nightshirt?"

He swatted his hand through the air. "I don't want that woman near me. She scrubs so hard she could rub smooth the back of an alligator."

Carina grinned. There was truth in that statement. Until she was old enough to wash herself, she'd just resigned herself to having red skin from Betsey's scrubbing during her weekly bath time. Her smile faded as she remembered her dilemma. "I can have Enoch or Woodson come up and give you a bucket bath."

"Woodson! He's not a house servant. Why, his hands are as rough as oak bark. Send Amos to me, and do it quick."

78

Her fader crossed his arms and glared at her. Carina swallowed hard. She'd made a decision for the welfare of all, and now she'd have to face the consequences. If she ever hoped to inherit Tanglewood—and there was nothing she wanted more, save the welfare of her servants—she had to prove to her fader that she was capable. She sucked in a strengthening breath and straightened her back. "Amos isn't here. He's gone."

"Gone!" Her fader bolted upright off the stack of pillows he'd been reclining on. "Did he go and run off? Who'd you hire to find him?" He scooted to the side of the bed and swung his legs over the edge, more nimbly than she'd seen him move in months.

She rushed to his side, uncertain if he could stand if he tried. How long had it been since he'd left his bed? She reached out to halt him. "Now, Fader, you are in no condition to get up."

He raised his elbow and shoved her back so hard she stumbled. She stepped on the hem of her skirt and fell on her backside, the fabric beneath her ripping. Tears pooled, but she forced them away. This was her only decent skirt.

Her fader scowled at her. For too long, she'd let him intimidate her and order her around as if she were one of his workers. She was his daughter—and the only reason he still had a home. She gathered her tattered skirts and ragged dignity and stood.

She pierced her fader with a glare. "Amos did not run away. I leased him and five other of our people to Mr. Davies for six months."

The left side of his face puckered up. "Lease? Zimmers don't lease their slaves. I'll be the laughingstock of Charleston."

She feared he was already ill-thought of by most of the people who knew him. Before he took ill, he was never kind.

He took anything he could take and never gave an inch. Many times she wished he had died instead of her mother or Johan. She hung her head at the insensitive thought. What kind of daughter was she?

Her fader scooted back into bed, launching a rank odor her way. He certainly needed a bath. "Tomorrow, you will go to Davies's business and tell him the deal is off. Bring back our slaves, you hear me?"

She hiked her chin. "I can't do that. Mr. Davies and I signed a contract. We need the money for the mortgage payment and supplies. For seed. We can manage without the extra help and will save food by having less mouths to feed during this difficult time."

Karl Zimmer's face grew as red as the borscht he loved so much. "I'm still the owner of this plantation. What makes you think you can do whatever you please?"

Carina winced. Her legs trembled, but she knew she had to stay the course and not back down. Her fader never respected anyone who caved to his hollering. "You're no longer physically able to run this plantation. I've done what I had to and made choices only after considerable thought and discussion with Betsey and Woodson."

"Discussion! With slaves?" He grabbed one of his pillows and lobbed it at her. "Slaves don't know squat. You can't discuss with them. That just shows you aren't fit to run this place."

"Neither are you." She nearly gasped out loud at her disrespectfulness. Never had she stood up to her fader before. "Someone has to make the decisions around here, and I'm the only one who can. You drink yourself half to death every day. A drunken man can't run a plantation." She took a step back, shocked at her tirade and half-afraid of what he would do to her. Thank the Lord he wasn't able to walk.

His face grew crimson, and he sputtered. "I don't know why Johan had to die instead of you." He reached under a pillow and pulled out one of his empty bottles and flung it at her.

Carina spun sideways and ducked, but she wasn't fast enough. The spiraling bottle crashed into her forehead, sending pain ratcheting through her. Her fader's face blurred then all turned black.

☙

Reed never thought he'd ever want to throttle another man, but if not for the fact that he was a God-fearing man, he was certain he would have laid his hands on Karl Zimmer—ill or not. How could a father be so cruel as to throw a heavy bottle at his daughter's head?

He tied off the last suture and snipped it.

"Is Miz 'Rina gonna be all right?" Betsey wrung her thick hands together and watched him from the far side of the bed.

"I hope so. I'll certainly do all I can to help her." He poured a generous amount of brandy over the wound to clean it then placed a square of cloth over it and wrapped Carina's head to hold it snug. He was grateful that she hadn't awakened during the suturing procedure, but the longer she was unconscious, the more concerned he became. *Please, Father, let her be all right. Heal her, Lord.*

He breathed in a long breath and straightened, rubbing the small of his back. He'd done all he knew to do. Now she was in God's hands. Reed turned down the lantern, knowing Carina would most likely be sensitive to light when she awoke since she had a head wound.

Betsey waddled around the bed and pulled a side chair from a desk across the room and dragged it toward him. She set it next to the bed. "You sit, Doctah Boss, and I'll go fetch you some tea and a slice of my buttermilk pie."

He smiled. "That sounds wonderful. It's been awhile since I ate anything."

Reed settled in, planning to stay until he knew Carina was faring well. The frayed curtains danced on the light breeze, while tree frogs, crickets, and other insects serenaded the moon as it made its way across the night sky. He laid his head against the ladder-back chair and closed his eyes, reliving the moment Enoch had come to his door and said that Miss Zimmer had been injured.

His first thought was of the dueling pistols, but he quickly cast that aside and asked Enoch what had happened. Reed clenched his back teeth, angered again at the unfair circumstances Carina was forced to endure. And a good measure of her suffering was his fault.

He longed to be her friend, to help her, but he doubted she'd be receptive. He slid his hand down her forearm to her slender wrist and checked her pulse. Breathing a sigh of relief, he boldly slid his hand into hers and held it. Hers was small, though not soft like his mother's, but rather callused, and her nails were chipped, rough. What kind of work had she done to earn those calluses? Reed pursed his lips, hesitated a moment, then placed a kiss on her index finger. Some way, somehow, he would make things easier for her.

Releasing her hand, he sat back and placed one hand over his chest. He'd do well to remember his patient's vendetta. She would not be happy to awaken and find him in her bedchamber, even with Betsey present, too. He rested his elbows on his knees and stared at the floor. He'd give Carina until he finished his tea and pie. If she hadn't awakened by then, he'd use smelling salts, but he preferred that a patient come to on their own.

Standing, he stretched and walked to the window, gazing out at the near-full moon. If his presence upset her, he'd go downstairs and supervise her from there. His mind whirled with ideas as to what he could do to help her. She was a neighbor and injured. He now had a legitimate excuse to come to her home and help out. Neighbors helped neighbors during times of trouble.

Once Carina was out of the woods, he'd put together a team of his servants and start clearing her drive. Maybe if it was more inviting, other neighbors would feel compelled to stop by for a visit.

A rustling sounded behind him, and he turned, checking Carina. Betsey shuffled through the door, carrying a tray with a huge slice of pie, a teapot, cup, and a small sugar bowl and creamer. She set the load on top of the desk and blew out a loud sigh. "I declare, those steps get taller and taller ever' day."

Reed's stomach growled in response to the sweet scent of the pie, and a warm cup of tea might help him to relax. But he doubted it. He wouldn't truly relax until Carina opened her eyes and yelled at him to leave. He smiled at that thought.

Betsey chuckled low and deep as she poured his tea. "Guess that pie arrived just in time."

He crossed the room and claimed the pie, cutting into it, then savoring the sweet flavor. "This is delicious. With desserts like this, I don't know how Miss Zimmer stays so thin."

"Hmpf." The colored woman crossed her arms across her ample bosom and plopped back down in the chair on the far side of the bed. "That's because she don't eat nuthin'."

"And why is that?" Though thinner than most women he knew, she seemed healthy enough. She'd never been faint or ill in his presence. In fact, she'd always had plenty of gumption and fortitude, enough to chase him off her land if need be. He couldn't help smiling as he remembered her ordering him off her land. No sir, Miss Carina Zimmer sure didn't lack fortitude and determination.

"I think she don't eat so we have more food." Betsey shook her head. "I fuss and fret, but nothing I can do will make Miz 'Rina eat another bite once she decides she's done."

"Maybe she'll eat if the doctor orders her to."

"And maybe she'll hop out of that bed and chase you off with her shotgun again."

Reed grinned and shook his head. "You're a sassy thing—you know it."

"I know." Betsey smiled and ducked her head. He doubted she'd ever talked to Mr. Zimmer so freely.

Reed finished his pie then downed his tea. He checked Carina's pulse again then paced the room for several minutes.

"Walkin' a hole in the carpet ain't gonna make her wake up no faster."

He sat back down and crossed one leg over his knee. His foot jiggled and he tapped the leg of the chair with his index finger. His gaze traveled around the room. The only furniture was the bed, desk, two chairs, and a commode with a chipped pitcher sitting in a ceramic bowl. Three pegs hung on the wall—one was empty, one held the shirtwaist he'd seen Carina wear several times, and the other held a faded brown dress with small yellow flowers. The sparseness of the room and her wardrobe put him to shame.

Betsey hummed a tune under her breath while she stitched up a tear in the ugly skirt Carina always wore.

"Why doesn't she have more clothing?"

Betsey's brows lifted in a manner that told him he'd overstepped his bounds. She glanced at her sleeping mistress then back at him. "Ever' time we get new fabric, Miz 'Rina, she says it has to go to someone else 'cause they needs it worse'n her, but that ain't the truth. She won't let me make her a new dress or skirt. She just wears this nasty old thing."

"What if the doctor ordered it burned for the sake of her health?"

Betsey smiled widely. "I like how you think, Doctah Boss, but there ain't nuthin' to replace this with." She held up the sad-looking skirt.

"Maybe my mother could help."

The slave woman pressed her lips together and shook her head. "Miz 'Rina, she don't like to accept he'p from others. She gots to do ever'thing herself."

Reed's admiration for the stubborn, independent woman kept rising. She placed her slaves before herself, worked her fingers to the bone to keep Tanglewood running while also tending an ailing father. "What exactly is wrong with Mr. Zimmer?"

Betsey lifted one shoulder then dropped it back down. "Don't rightly know. He took to his bed after a sickness over a year ago and nevah got up again—at least not when nobody is lookin'."

Leaning forward on his arms, Reed glanced at Carina again then focused on her maid. "You're saying he can get out of bed when he wants to?"

"I'm not sayin' nuthin'." She pressed her lips together and shook her head then glanced at the door and leaned toward Reed. "Just that he don't treat his daughter good. She works from sunup to past dark ever' day, and he don't lift a hand to he'p. He just moans and groans, drinks that liquor all day, and pines away for that no-good son of his. Would be better for all if he just up and died."

"I should check on him while I'm here."

Betsey's eyes went wide and she waved her hand in the air. "Oh no, sir, he wouldn't like that none. He hates Bishops even more'n Miz 'Rina."

Reed ducked his head, not wanting her to see how her words had wounded him. He didn't want Carina to hate him. He wanted to be her friend. *Please, Lord, soften her heart toward me. Make her willing to let me help her.*

He considered his plan again. Those limbs that hung over the drive were dangerous. If one was to fall when someone was riding under them, a person could get killed or seriously injured. First thing when he returned home, he would set his plan into action.

ten

Carina fought the darkness, searching for the voice that called to her. Where was she? Why was the fog so thick?

A strip of light appeared in the distance, and she clawed her way toward it, though it pained her eyes fiercely. And her head—the pressure, the pain—was a horse sitting on it?

"Come on, Carina, wake up."

Someone squeezed her hand. The touch felt odd—unfamiliar, but welcomed. Reassuring.

"That's it, come on."

Now her hand was encased between two big, warm hands, guiding, leading her across the dark abyss to the light. To him.

She blinked and saw Betsey stand and hurry toward her. Glancing up, she recognized the cracked plaster of her bedroom ceiling—a large, spiderlike web creeping across the ceiling and down the walls. Why was she in bed in the middle of the day? What had happened?

Lifting her hand, she found the reason for the pressure in her head. A tightly wrapped bandage. "Off. Hurts."

A gentle hand pulled hers back. "Sorry, but the bandage needs to stay on for a few days. You've had an accident, and you have an inch-long gash that I had to suture."

Carina scowled and turned toward the man's voice. Brilliant blue eyes laced with concern stared down at her. Reed Bishop's eyes. What was he doing in her room?

She pushed up in the bed, causing pain to radiate through her head, then clutched her forehead, unable to hold back a groan.

Mr. Bishop stood. "I'll give her some laudanum for the pain. Would you mind bringing some more hot water, Betsey? We can mix it with some tea."

Nodding, the maid rose and hurried to the doorway. "Etta! Bring up some hot water."

"Ow, don't holler." Carina squeezed her eyes shut, partly because of the pain and partly so she didn't have to look at *him*.

The doctor picked up her wrist and held on to it. "Good. Your pulse is steady and strong. Tell me how you're feeling. Is there anything you want?"

She wanted him to hold her hand again, to coo those soft words of encouragement again, and to tell her everything would be fine. But it wouldn't. Never. Last night had proven that no matter how hard she worked or what she did, she could never replace her brother. That she could never earn her fader's approval. How would she find the strength to go on? Maybe it would have been better if she'd never awakened.

"What's wrong? Is the pain severe?"

"Why do you care?" She pulled the light quilt up to her neck. "Why are you here?"

"Betsey sent for me when you were injured, and I came right away. A head wound is nothing to take lightly."

She didn't want to be beholden to him. She couldn't pay him for his services. Turning her face to the wall, she spoke what she felt he wanted to hear. "Well, you've treated me, so now you're free to go."

"I'm the doctor, Miss Zimmer. I'll be the one who decides when to take my leave."

Inwardly, she was glad that he didn't back down, but she knew she shouldn't be. Why would he of all people be the one to comfort her—to make her feel better? She should be angry still, but she was just too tired. She'd lost her will to fight. Her heavy eyelids weighed too much, and she couldn't resist the pull of sleep. Maybe when she awakened, she would discover this was all a bad dream.

&

Reed paced the piazza and stared across the front lawn—a weed patch, actually—and down the drive. Clearing all the debris and getting this place looking decent again would take many men and a lot of muscle. He didn't mind helping a neighbor in need—it was the way of life in the South—but what was one to do when said neighbor didn't want help?

A grin tugged at his lips. He was the doctor and could order Miss Zimmer to stay in bed for several days, which she should anyway. If he got together a large enough crew and recruited help from his cousin, just maybe they could get the drive cleared before the obstinate woman found out.

He contemplated the distance. Would she be able to hear them working? If they started at the entrance near the main road first and worked their way toward the house, they could probably get most of the job done before she caught wind of it. He rapped his palms on the porch railing, liking the idea more and more. Might be a good idea to mention it to Woodson so he didn't come after them with an ax.

The door opened, and his mother stepped out. She'd arrived early, right after the breakfast hour, with a basket of fragrant goodies on her arm.

He nodded to her. "Are you satisfied Miss Zimmer will live?"

Grinning, she wrapped her arm around his waist. "I never had a doubt, not when she had the care of such a fine doctor."

Her praise warmed his heart. Even though her greatest desire was for him to be a planter as his father had been, she still had the grace to encourage him in his dream.

"I'm not so sure she'll be able to live down her embarrassment of you being in her room and seeing her in her nightgown though." She glanced up at him with a stern look. "You didn't help Betsey get her changed out of her dress, did you?"

"I'm a doctor, Mother. Things like that don't affect me."

She studied his face. "Don't be telling me whoppers, son."

He grinned and lifted his gaze to see Sammy zigzagging along the side of the barn, chasing butterflies. "I did not help with that. Etta assisted her mother in getting Miss Zimmer into her nightgown."

"Well, I'm relieved to know you still have some sense of decency."

He enjoyed the playful banter but was glad he'd skirted the truth. Seeing capable Carina lying there bleeding and unconscious had just about been his undoing. Would she despise him all over again because she'd have a scar where he'd stitched her wound? It would have been far worse and taken much longer to heal if he hadn't sutured the gaping injury.

"She'll be fine, son, though her dignity may be fragile for a bit, especially when you're around. Carina doesn't like people helping her."

"And why is that?"

She turned to face him and crossed her arms. "She's had to be strong, independent, all her life. She lost her mother at such a young age and had a younger brother who looked up to her all his life. Her father uprooted them from their home and brought them here. Karl never should have become a planter. His trade was watchmaking, but he had lofty visions of leaving Boston to live in a warmer climate and grow crops. Karl never had the fortitude nor the proper knowledge to run a large plantation, and he wasn't willing to learn from his neighbors when they offered sage advice."

"Karl? You know him well enough to refer to him by his first name?"

She pursed her lips and nodded. "Yes. Your father befriended him when he first moved here. I came with him a few times because I felt sorry for Karl's motherless children, but I didn't like how he looked at me when your father's gaze was occupied elsewhere."

Reed narrowed his gaze. The more he heard about Karl Zimmer, the less he liked. "I should check on him, but Betsey doesn't think he'd be receptive."

"It would be a good thing if you tried."

He nodded, knowing the doctor in him really gave him no choice. He'd check on both Mr. Zimmer and Abel before leaving today. Sammy gave up chasing butterflies and hunkered down like a bobcat, trailing a yellow cat into the barn. In the paddock on the far side of the barn, Lulu ambled along, stretching her head below the lowest rail in search of grass on the other side.

"I've made a couple of decisions. I plan to buy a good horse and also to hire a carpenter to build a clinic near the road."

His mother's chin lifted slightly. "It's good you've decided what you want to do." Her words belied what she truly felt.

"I thought I'd have a bell installed that could be rung to alert me when someone had arrived at the clinic. That way I can be at home when I'm not needed there."

Her head jerked toward him, her gaze hopeful. "Does that mean you intend to oversee the plantation, too?"

After learning of Carina's sacrifices for her home, how could he do less? He hadn't considered how much of a burden it must have been for his mother to make all the decisions of the plantation by herself. "Yes, Mama. I'm sorry for not seeing how much of a burden that was on you sooner."

She smiled and leaned her head against his shoulder. Her silence and the way she hugged his arm spoke volumes. For far too long he'd played around and had fun with his friends. It was time he stepped up and became the man of his home.

But when he thought of his home, it seemed incomplete. Something was missing. His mother hadn't pressed him, but he knew for certain that she'd been scouring the community in search of just the right woman for him to marry. She would expect him to give her an heir before too long. Was he ready for marriage and fatherhood?

His thoughts drifted back to Carina. Dared he hope she could ever come to have feelings for him?

God could work mighty miracles, but he was afraid to believe that even the good Lord could effect such a drastic change in Miss Zimmer's heart.

❧

For days, a ceaseless pounding had assaulted Carina's head. Only at night did it lessen. She hated being abed for so long when so many things needed attending, but when she'd tried to rise, her vision blurred and swam around the room. Betsey and Etta had delivered meal after meal and stuffed her like a roasted hen with broth, bread, and porridge for the past three days. Though she rarely ate much at most mealtimes, she was hankering for something more substantial. A thick beef or venison steak sounded more to her liking than broth.

With her puny breakfast over, she was bound and determined to get out of bed. She sat up, glad that the awful dizziness seemed to have passed. Scooting sideways, she dangled her legs over the side of the bed and waited. When nothing happened, she eased off the side and stood. Her legs trembled from lack of use, and the dull pain in her head intensified. But the pounding she'd heard now sounded as if it were coming from outside. She inched toward the window, hoping her legs wouldn't give out, and she finally latched onto the frame. Her limbs were more wobbly than a newborn filly's.

She peered outside, past the barn, looking for Woodson and Enoch. What could they be doing to make so much noise? As far as she could tell, neither man was working in the field. A loud crack, like an explosion, sounded off to the southwest, and she spun her head in that direction. From her viewpoint, she could only see the part of the drive closest to the house. The noise sounded farther away. Could it be coming from the Bishop plantation?

She had to know, even if she had to walk across the hall to find out.

"Jes' what do you think yo're doin', missy?" Betsey stood in the doorway, filling the whole opening. Her chest rose and fell at a frantic pace, as it always did right after she'd climbed the stairs.

"It's time I was up. There's plenty of work that needs doing." Her talk was bold, but she glanced back at the chair, needing to sit before she collapsed. She didn't want Betsey to see her weakness.

"Either you sit down or get back in the bed." Pushing past Carina, Betsey hurried to the desk, pulled out the chair, then gave her a no-nonsense glare.

Trying to fool Betsey was a waste of time. She grabbed hold of the chair's back, while her maid took hold of her other arm and helped her down. "Sometimes I wonder who's the boss around here."

"There's a new boss around these days." Grinning, Betsey crossed to the bed and yanked off the sheets. "These could use a good washin'."

"I could use a good washing." Carina grinned. "And what did you mean about there being a *new* boss? Are you talking about Woodson? Or you?"

Betsey mumbled something about uppity white folks, but Carina knew she was only teasing. "We'd best get you washed up. Mrs. Bishop, she done told me she'd come back to visit midmornin'."

Carina didn't miss how her maid had avoided her question, but she simply didn't have the energy to pursue an answer. And Susan was returning. Her first inclination was to decline the visit, but in truth, she had enjoyed her time with Mr. Bishop's mother yesterday, and she'd even found Susan's reading of the scriptures a comfort. It was Susan's son who set her on edge. She glanced down at her hand and rubbed her fingers together. The man she'd attempted to kill had turned around and doctored her, comforted her, and caressed her hand. She'd treated him so horribly, yet one would never have known by the way he'd acted. Was it merely the doctor in him that was able to push aside a personal offense to so meticulously care for the very person who'd inflicted the pain? Or was there more to it?

Betsey grabbed the pitcher off the commode. "I'll be back with some hot water, so you just sit there and don't do nuthin'. If you need somethin', holler for me or Etta—she be downstairs dustin'." Turning, she bustled out the door, mumbling something about "that girl" under her breath.

Carina laid her head back against the chair and concentrated on the look she remembered in Dr. Bishop's caring gaze. He had seemed worried, as if he truly cared about her. But how could that be possible? Hadn't he shown the same compassion for Abel?

She stood and walked back to the window, feeling a bit stronger. Susan had told her how much her son had changed in the time he'd been gone. How becoming a Christian had changed him from a selfish, spoiled boy to a gentle, caring man. Leaning her head against the window frame, she wondered if that was true. Was Susan just a proud mother, overemphasizing her son's positive traits?

Betsey's labored footsteps plodded down the hall in her direction. Could she talk to her about Dr. Bishop? She heaved a sigh. Probably not. Her maid had fallen in love with him the day he splinted Abel's leg, and now Betsey's feelings had surely grown like bread dough on a warm day since he'd taken such good care of her.

Rather than dreading her next encounter with Reed Bishop, she looked forward to it. Was there any hope they might become friends? Was she willing to turn loose of her bitterness to make that happen?

Even if she did, how could he ever forget how she had treated him?

And what about Johan? Could it possibly be true her brother had started the duel?

She shook her head. She didn't have a prayer of a chance that a Zimmer and a Bishop could ever make peace.

eleven

Reed wiped the sweat from his eyes. The scene playing out before him made him proud to be a Southerner. He'd put out the call—that Carina Zimmer had been injured—and people from most of the neighboring plantations had either come to help or sent a crew of workers. Along with the dozen men he'd rounded up from Reed Springs, the total numbered more than twenty-five at last count. Saws swished, hoes whacked, and the colored folks serenaded everyone with soul-touching spirituals.

A bevy of the females, both white and Negro, had set up camp under a huge live oak and a batch of stew was simmering over a campfire. A couple of men had set up tables in the shade for them, and several other ladies were setting out cups of cider and water for the meal. Women who weren't cooking sat on a blanket talking and sewing. This was more than a chance to help a hurting neighbor; it was an opportunity for community—for friends and even some family—to spend time together.

The difference they'd made was astounding. Dead limbs had been removed and cut up for firewood, which Enoch had been hauling up to the house. All the vines that had tangled around trees and begun to choke the life out of them were gone, shrubs trimmed or removed. Why, the next time he rode over to Tanglewood, he might accidentally ride right past the entrance because it looked so different.

Carina needed a sign with her plantation's name on it, and

he could make one. He wondered what she would say when she saw what they had done. Would she be happy—or angry?

Reed's cousin caught his eye and waved. Seth pulled a bandanna from his waistband and swiped his face as Reed approached. "Taking a break already?"

"Already!" Seth gazed up at the sky. "By my calculations, it's almost quitting time."

Reed's stomach growled, as if in agreement. He gazed past the last of the workers to the final curve in the road. Once they rounded that point, anyone at the house could see them. He was somewhat surprised that Carina hadn't come stomping down the road with her shotgun, ordering them off her property.

"What's wrong? You look nervous."

Shrugging, Reed turned back to his cousin. "Just wondering what Miss Zimmer will say to all this."

Seth frowned. "How could she not be pleased?"

Reed walked ahead three feet, picked up a large stick, and tossed it in the back of the rubbish wagon. "It's a difficult situation. She hasn't had anyone to rely on and has managed to run the plantation and care for her ailing father all by herself."

"What's wrong with her father?"

Shrugging, Reed stared back at the house. "I tried to examine Mr. Zimmer, but he just lambasted me and sent me from his room. I have my suspicions that it may just be the drink that is incapacitating him—that and his bad attitude about all things."

"Hmm. . .I see what you mean. Must be hard for Miss Zimmer to live here alone and never see other people."

Reed nodded. "If I have my way about it, I plan on changing that."

Seth's green eyes twinkled. "Do I detect a blossoming romance?"

"Ha!" Reed barked such a loud laugh that several people turned to see what was so funny. "If there was such a thing, it would be decidedly one-sided." He lifted his hat and fanned his sweaty face. His gaze followed a man with a scruffy beard and ragged, loose-fitting clothes as he wandered along the edge of the work area closest to the food tables.

"What do you make of him?" He nodded with his chin toward the man.

Seth shook his head. "Never saw him before. Must work for another planter."

Reed continued watching the man. He'd done little work today, although if one weren't watching too closely it wouldn't have been noticed. The man ambled along, picking up a vine or twig here and there, his gaze continually flicking back to the food table, where the women almost had the meal ready. Reed's mouth watered.

And where was his mother? She'd promised to come down and help oversee the food preparations. Even as the thought fled his mind, he saw her walking down the road, a basket over her arm with Betsey and Etta close behind her. She looked every bit the mistress of the plantation. He was partly relieved Miss Zimmer hadn't come, too, but on the other hand, he was anxious to see her again. Excited to show her what her neighbors had accomplished. Wary to see her reaction. Would life with Miss Zimmer always be a constant ebb and flow of emotions and desires?

He walked out to greet his mother and relieved her of her basket. He nodded to Betsey and Etta. "How's my patient today?"

Betsey shook her head. "Fussy. Grumblin' to get up. Don't

know how much longer I can keep her down."

"Are you sure she can't start moving around some—maybe leave her room? She's about to go crazier than a chicken in a rain barrel." His mother glanced up at him and smiled. She might be sweet, but she was a Southern lady and had no reservations about using her feminine wiles to sway him to her side.

He hadn't seen Carina in two days, so he needed to check on her anyway. "I'll stop by when we're done here and assess how she is doing."

"Mind that you wash up first." His mother's gaze ran down his dirty shirt and trousers. The shine that had been on his boots this morning was buried under a layer of dust. He wasn't in much of a state to go visiting, but then he wasn't going to impress a lady, but rather to check on a patient.

Seth slugged his arm. "Hey, look over there."

Reed turned and glanced in the direction his cousin pointed. The thin man with the scruffy beard they'd discussed earlier grabbed a whole loaf of bread and shoved it into his satchel. He glanced right and left, slid over to another table near a tree, and leaned on it, while his gaze darted all over. Reed looked back at Seth so the man wouldn't see him staring. "Is he doing what I think?"

"Look!" His mother gasped. "Why—that man is stealing that slab of ham!" She waved her hand in the air as if trying to flag down a runaway wagon. "Somebody, hey! Stop that man."

"C'mon." Reed yanked on Seth's shirt. If the skinny man they'd seen earlier was hungry, all he had to do was tell somebody, and they'd willingly give him food. But to steal it, that was something that couldn't be tolerated. He kicked up his pace, but the thief darted into the wooded area surrounding the swamp. With Seth on his heels, Reed dodged in and out of tree after tree, but the wiry man knew just which way to go to elude him. Finally Reed stopped and leaned over, resting his hands on his knees as he struggled to catch a breath.

As his breathing slowed and the thundering in his ears subsided, all he could hear was Seth's loud breaths beside him and the normal sounds of the swamp—the swish of the Spanish moss on the gentle breeze in the trees overhead, a loud splash in the pond's inky water to his right. Songbirds serenaded the treetops, insects hummed, and a chorus of frogs joined the symphony.

Swamp grass, a myriad of trees and bushes met his gaze, but not a person other than his cousin. How had that man just disappeared?

"He's gone. Let's head back. I'm starving."

Reed nodded. "Just let me wash off in the pond." Stooping beside the bank, he searched the area near the shore, making sure no gators were hovering close by. He wouldn't be the first man surprised by one of those big creatures lurking just under the surface of the water. He dipped in his hands and swished them around, washing the day's grime off.

Seth nudged Reed's backside with his leg. "Watch out for the swamp monster." He chuckled.

Reed finished splashing water on his face then rinsed his hands. As a doctor, he preferred being cleaner and washing his hands more frequently than most men did. He stood and shook his damp hair on Seth. "You need a bath, cousin. You're pungent."

"Hey!" Seth gave him a playful push.

They headed back, neither talking. Reed thought about how they'd played as kids around the swamp at Reed Springs and also neighboring Madison Gardens, where Seth had grown up. He hadn't thought of the swamp monster in years. Those had been fun times.

"I guess we need to ask around and see who that fellow works for. Maybe they'll know where he's run off to."

Reed nodded his agreement as they broke through the tree line. The four planters from the surrounding plantations who'd been helping all day headed his way.

"Looks like that thief got away." Mason Dugger stared past Reed as if waiting for the man to walk out of the woods.

"He seemed to know the swamp area quite well, and he was fast." Reed looked from man to man. "Which one of you does he work for?"

Each of the planters cast accusing glances at one another. Finally Peter Reynolds shook his head. "Not me. Never saw him before."

The others followed suit, each denying having hired the man. Had the thief been hiding in the woods and taken advantage of the situation? Had he heard about the gathering and come to help in order to eat? Not that he'd been all that much help. Reed rubbed the back of his neck, not liking Carina being so defenseless in that big house without a man close by to help if needed. Of course, Betsey would probably come running and wallop an intruder with her iron skillet—if she could catch him.

"What's so funny? Is there something you're not telling us?" Seth stared at Reed like he'd taken leave of his senses.

Sobering, he shook his head. "I just had a thought. I'm concerned about both the Zimmers being injured and no able-bodied man in the house, should the thief decide to break in."

John Bowman grunted. "She can get one of her slaves to stay on the porch and keep watch all night." He turned and sauntered back to the food tables, where people had started filling their plates. As if the issue had been settled, the others also turned and headed back to their meal, all except for Seth and William Dean, a newcomer to the area. Dean was a hard worker—a widower with two children, Reed had heard, even though the man was only a few years older than Reed.

He scanned the area and located Woodson and Enoch, still loading wood into the wagon. What his friends didn't know was that Carina only had one other male servant besides those two. She was down to a bare minimum of workers and couldn't afford to have one of them stay up all night keeping watch. Sammy would volunteer, he was certain, but it wasn't likely the boy could stay awake all night, and besides, he'd be precious little help when confronted by a grown man on a mission.

"That Mrs. Zimmer must be a widow, huh?"

Reed's gaze jerked back to Mr. Dean. The widower would probably be considered a handsome man to most women with his blond hair and brown eyes. He was about the same six-foot-tall height as Reed, but the planter was much broader in the shoulders. Didn't women prefer men with big shoulders? He straightened and glanced at Seth, who shrugged and grinned. "Why do you ask, Mr. Dean?"

He swatted his hand in the air. "Call me Will or Willy. Aren't you the new doctor? Sure glad to have one closer than Charleston."

Reed nodded, relaxing under the man's welcoming smile. His straight, white teeth would probably be another factor in his favor with females. Reed touched the end of his front tooth with his tongue, the tooth that was missing a corner from when he fell and smacked his face on Cook's worktable, years ago.

Will nodded. "And I believe in being straight with folks. I've got me a young boy and girl who need a mama. I'm looking to marry again. Don't much care for being alone." His gaze searched the crowd and landed in the area where Reed's mother was passing out slices of bread to the men in line. "She's a fine-looking woman, although a bit older than I expected. You think she's open to marrying again?"

Reed clenched his jaw. Surely Will must be looking at someone other than his mother.

Seth turned with obvious curiosity in the direction Will was looking. "Which lady are you talking about?"

Will smiled widely and pointed straight at Reed's mother. "That one there in the pretty purple dress with the brownish hair. Hat tied under her chin with the big bow. Isn't that Mrs. Zimmer? I saw her walking from the house with two of her servants."

Seth sputtered and doubled over. "Ho, ho! That's hilarious."

Reed narrowed his eyes.

Will looked at Seth as if he'd turned green and grown six horns. "What's so funny? I need a wife, and it doesn't matter to me if she's a bit older, as long as she'd be kind to my children. Nothing humorous about it."

"A *bit* older?" Reed ground out between clenched teeth.

Will swung around and took another look. "Well, maybe a tad more than a bit, but she's still a fine-looking woman. How old do you reckon she is? Thirty-two, maybe?"

Seth slapped his leg and laughed so hard tears ran down his cheeks. Will blinked, obviously confused, while the people closest to them turned to see what was going on.

"That woman is not interested in getting married."

Will's chin lifted slightly. "How do you know? Have you already approached her?"

Seth roared with laughter and fell down to his knees. He cackled like an old hen then snorted and gasped for a breath.

Will shook his head. "What—is—so—funny?"

Reed wanted to be angry, but the humor of the situation overpowered his irritation with the misguided man. "That is not *Miss* Zimmer. That woman you're admiring is my mother."

Seth snorted and managed to get up on his knees. His cheeks were wet with his tears. "Yeah, and she's twenty years your senior."

Will looked at Reed. "Oh." Then he glanced down at Seth. "Oh." Suddenly he puffed up, his cheeks the color of the filling of Mrs. Bowman's cherry pie. He nodded at Reed. "My apologies. I should probably be getting back to my children. Left 'em with their mammy." He slapped his hat back onto his head and marched to his horse, stiff and proud.

Seth continued to chuckle. Reed nudged him with the toe of his boot. "Not a word of this to Mother, you hear me?"

Seth pressed his lips together, but he was still laughing, if his bouncing shoulders were any indication.

Reed held out his hand for his cousin, and Seth took it, allowing Reed to help him up. Seth wiped his eyes and grinned. "I wish you could have seen your face. I don't know, though. Were you upset because he confused your mama for Miss Zimmer, or because Will is looking to marry and isn't too picky?" Seth glanced over his shoulder to where one could see a corner of the upstairs of the Zimmer home; then he caught Reed's gaze. "You know that you just confirmed to Dean that Miss Zimmer isn't married, don't you? When you emphasized she was a miss." He smacked Reed on the shoulder. "Don't dawdle too long. If you've got designs on Miss Zimmer, cousin, I wouldn't wait long to tell her."

Reed's jaw dropped as Seth strode toward the tables. How did he know that Reed liked Carina, when he barely knew it himself? He glanced in the direction of the house. Maybe he should stay a night or two to make sure things were all right. Tomorrow his men and Carina's could finish the drive's manicure project. Then maybe he'd take her for a short buggy ride and show her what all her neighbors had done.

He just hoped she wouldn't be so upset that she'd pull out her pistol again and fire it at him this time.

twelve

Carina was going to shoot Reed Bishop. She'd hoped this could be a new beginning between her and the doctor, not to mention a chance to finally get out of the house, but the day had suddenly plummeted downhill like a runaway buggy. He hadn't even noticed that she was wearing the new skirt his mother had helped her sew the past few days from some unused fabric she had stuffed in a wardrobe.

She stared at her trees—chopped, sawed, and whittled back into submission. The horrid vines that had threatened to choke the life out of her bushes and trees were gone. There were even wheel tracks pressing down the weeds in the road. It looked nice, actually. In fact, she couldn't remember when it had ever looked so orderly.

"Well?" Reed nudged her shoulder with his, a proud twinkle in his eye. "You going to say anything?"

She faced him on the seat—the very narrow seat. His cheek was less than a foot from hers. She swallowed. "Part of me is furious. How could you do such a thing without my knowledge, and how did you get it done so fast?"

"Had some help."

"You must have had a whole lot of help. Who was it?"

He pulled in his lips and looked off to the side, giving her a moment to study him. His cheeks had a pleasing tan, not the pale color of so many businessmen from the city. His nose was straight and just the right size—not too big or too small. Today his clothes were dirty from his physical labors, not spotless as on most occasions. She actually preferred this more casual look. His hair hung down to his shoulders, damp and curling from a recent washing. She exhaled a sigh. Why did they always have to be at odds with one another?

He turned back to her, his eyes pleading for understanding. "I. . .uh. . .told some. . .uh. . .neighbors about your being injured and how you needed some help."

"What!" She shot to her feet, conking her head on the top of the buggy. Rubbing the sore spot, she glared down at him. "I do not need help, Dr. Bishop. I've told you before that Zimmers take care of themselves. Who was it who helped, anyway?"

"Sit down before you fall off the buggy, please." He gently tugged on her arm.

She did as asked, but only because standing there with her neck bent so awkwardly due to the low roof made her head hurt. Folding her hands and clenching them, she listened as he rattled off a list of her neighbors who had come and helped clear her long drive. Her ire grew with each name that fell from his lips.

So many names. So many people to be beholden to. How could she possible pay them all back?

Now she understood what all the pounding had been about. It hadn't been her head at all—well, maybe some of it was at first, but not later. Even her fader had fussed about it, according to Betsey, but he merely drank more and spent the past few days in a stupor.

Carina allowed her gaze to wander down the closely cropped drive. It actually did look very nice. Maybe they could plant some flowers along the side of the road, but then that would require a lot more labor and someone to locate the plants and then water them. She sighed. Always more work.

"Tell me what you're thinking. Are you upset?"

The gentleness in his voice drew her, made her want to cast aside all her worries and trust him. But how could she ever truly trust a Bishop?

"Yes, I'm upset. Just think how many people I'm indebted to now—and I don't even know some of them. How could I ever repay them?"

He turned slightly in the seat, knocking his knees against her. "They don't expect repayment. They did it to help an injured neighbor."

"Why? Why now, when no one ever offered to help before?"

"Everyone needs help sometimes. Help from family. Help from friends, and help from God."

"You're avoiding my question, Dr. Bishop. Why help me? Why now?"

"Because I put out word that there was a need."

She glanced down at her hands. "Therein lies the truth. They came because *you* asked. You—a Bishop, descendant of the Reeds who helped establish Charleston and have lived in the area for more than one hundred years, so the story goes. It had nothing to do with me or my father."

His arm slipped around behind her, resting lightly on the seat, almost an open invitation for her to scoot up close to him, but she didn't move. Could barely breathe.

"That's just the way of the South. Neighbors help neighbors. I realize it's harder for you to understand since you're not native to here, but accept their assistance and desire to help and be grateful that they did. I nearly got lost in those mangy trees and shrubs every time I rode home. Thought for sure one of these days a vine was going to shoot out, trip up my horse, and drag me into the swamp, never to be heard from again."

She giggled at the ridiculous image he painted. Glancing

up at him, her smile fled. The intensity in his eyes stole her breath. He reached up and smoothed a lock of hair behind her ear, so gentle, so different from her own father's cruel touch. She ducked her head and turned away.

Think of Johan. Think of all her fader had been through. She couldn't allow herself to get close to this man. Her fader would never allow her to marry a Bishop.

She shook her head. Marry? Where had that thought come from?

"I'm sorry you're not happy. I just wanted to help you."

"No, don't misunderstand. I do like the changes." She stared down the road then over her shoulder back toward the house, taking in everything. All trees and shrubs within three feet of either side of the road had been cut back or removed. Several piles of debris were placed every hundred feet or so.

"I've talked with Woodson, and he will burn those rubbish heaps tomorrow or the day after, depending on the winds. We were late finishing today, and folks needed to head home to tend to chores."

She nodded, amazed at the difference. "It looks very nice. I just. . ."

"Don't make things more than they are."

Her irritation fueled. He had no idea what it was like to be shunned. Not a single neighbor other than his mother had ever come to visit her. Not even after Johan died. She blinked back tears. "I appreciate your efforts, but those good people did this for you, not me. They don't even know me."

His arm lowered onto her shoulders and rested there, as light as a feather. "I think you're wrong. If they could get to know you, you'd see that. Why not get out and attend some of the local social events? Come to church when the itinerate pastor visits each month?"

She shook her head. Tanglewood was her private sanctuary. The only safe place. She didn't want to leave it. "I can't."

"Yes, you can." His arm tightened. "You can go with Mother and me."

She shook her head. He'd never understand what it was like to be the daughter of a man people despised—a man who had cheated his neighbors to benefit himself. A man who never forgot a wrong done to him. "Please, take me back home."

His heavy sigh sluiced guilt through her. He removed his arm and jiggled the reins, turning the horse back toward the house. He'd only been trying to help. She held her hands in her lap, wishing more than anything that things could be different.

"I'll be gone for the next few days."

His statement and the lifeless way it was uttered dug a hole in her heart. Why couldn't he understand? She had no way to repay anyone. Keeping the plantation running and growing enough food to feed her small crew along with caring for her fader took all her time and energy.

"I'm going to Charleston to purchase a horse and hire someone to build a clinic for me. Is there anything you need from there? I'd be happy to get it."

His offer to help was generous, all things considered. Generous, just like him. She had hated him for so long that she still had trouble reconciling the kindhearted Dr. Bishop with the hooligan she knew he'd been when he was younger. The lout who killed her brother.

He pulled the buggy to a stop, set the brake, and climbed out, then turned and held out his hands to her. Swallowing back her nervousness at touching him, she forced herself to move and stood, taking care not to bang her head again. She placed her hands on his shoulders, and he gently lifted her to the ground. When he didn't release her right away, she glanced up. Those eyes, so intense, so blue, seemed to look clear into her soul. What did he see? A woman who wished things could be different? A woman who was sorry for all that had happened between their families?

He let go and stepped back. "You may get up and move about the house now, but don't do any physical labor. If you start feeling dizzy, sit or lie down. And have Betsey change your bandage in a few days."

She hated the professionalism in his voice and the dullness of his eyes, as a man who'd lost all hope. What had he hoped to gain from her? Why hadn't he just stayed away? Stayed in Scotland?

Knowing him to be the sweet man he was now only made things so much more difficult. Just think of how he'd cut Johan's life short. Had her brother been here all these years, her life would not have been so hard. "Thank you for all you've done, Dr. Bishop. If you could be so kind as to provide me with a list of the people who worked on the drive, I would appreciate it. I'd like to pen them a thank-you note."

He gave a terse nod and held out his hand, helping her up the stairs. He opened the door for her. "I'll check on Abel before leaving. If he feels up to it, he can sit now and do simple tasks like polishing tack. Nothing that requires walking yet."

She nodded. "I understand."

"Another thing. Betsey has probably mentioned this by now, but there was a vagrant down where we were working. He stole some food then ran off into the swamp."

Carina's heart leaped. "Do you think he might come here?"

He pressed his lips together and shrugged. "I'm hoping he was just hungry and has moved on, but it might be a good idea to post a night guard for the next week or so."

That meant she'd be short another servant. She could hardly expect a man to stay up most of the night then work all day. But neither could she risk their safety or that of her property. She couldn't afford to lose so much as a shovel or a spoon. Crossing her arms, she ran her palms up and down her outer arms as she searched the fields and then the area around the barn. Was someone spying on them even now?

He lifted his gaze past her to the stairs leading to the second floor. "One more thing you should know, I attempted to examine your father yesterday, but he wanted nothing to do with me."

"Can you blame him?" She stiffened at the unexpected harshness in her voice. She hadn't meant to sound so bitter.

His lips pressed tightly together, a wounded look in his eyes. He ducked his head. "No, I don't suppose I can. My family has done nothing but cause him—and you—trouble. Please accept my sincere apologies, Miss Zimmer." He slapped his hat on his head, spun around, and jogged down the stairs, taking Carina's heart with him.

ð

Stubborn, mulish woman—beautiful woman.

Why couldn't she acknowledge what was happening between them? He knew she felt something, because her whole demeanor had changed. Her true anger had dissipated only to be replaced with a false, forced anger, as if she needed to hold on to it or lose her identity. If she liked him at all, why did she keep pushing him away? Had he completely misread her interest?

He'd almost kissed her in the buggy. What a mistake that would have been. He smacked the reins on the horse's back, and the animal jumped and leaped forward. Getting away from the beguiling Miss Zimmer was probably the smartest thing he could do. She wasn't some wounded animal he'd found out in a field or the barn, but a living, breathing person. He couldn't fix all her problems, and trying to wasn't God's will for his life. He was a doctor—and he needed a clinic.

He turned off the main road onto the quarter-mile drive that took him home, slowed, and studied the landscape. A beautiful valley spread before him with a backdrop of trees that hugged the river. This was the perfect spot for his clinic. Close to the main road, yet far enough away that the dust stirred up by travelers wouldn't drift into the windows. Maybe closer to the river would be better, so that he'd have quicker access to fresh water.

He tapped his lip and glanced around the field. Finally he nodded. "This is it."

thirteen

Carina sat in the rocker on the front porch, watching the smoke from the debris piles slowly change from black to gray. Thankfully, the wind had blown it away from the house all day.

Sammy raced around the corner and didn't stop until he reached the porch. He climbed up onto the railing instead of using the stairs and sucked in a breath, his dark eyes shining. "Daddy says to tell you that there's the last of the piles."

"Thank you for telling me." She wrinkled her nose. "You smell like you've been standing downwind of them."

He nodded. "I played in the smoke. Pretended I was an Indian." He jumped to the ground. "Daddy says I should go see to Abel. See if'n he needs somethun'." He loped away as fast as he'd come.

She shook her head, wishing she had his energy. Just two years past twenty and she was already tired. Maybe she just hadn't fully recovered from her injuries yet. But her discouragement was more than physical. Her heart ached. It probably would never heal, not after her fader's harsh words and treatment. She shelled the last of the peas in the bowl on her lap, blinking back unwanted tears. *Why couldn't you have died instead of Johan?*

Betsey banged her way out the front door. "You done shellin' those peas yet?"

She held up the bowl and gave her maid a proud smile. "All done."

"Took you 'bout as long as it does Etta."

Carina lifted her brows and couldn't resist teasing. "I've been injured."

"Hmpf. Ain't nuthin' wrong with yo' fingers." She stared off toward the road. "Guess Sammy and Woodson'll stink to high heaven when they gets home. Gonna have to go dunk 'em in the river."

Carina smiled. From what she'd heard from Sammy, the menfolk went for a swim most warm evenings. She wished she had that liberty, but she was always afraid of an alligator inviting her for dinner or someone seeing her. And lately, she kept getting the feeling she was being watched. Her gaze traveled around the yard, the barn, the paddock, and back to the road. Maybe her head wound was the cause of her insecurity of late.

"Sure do miss Doctah Boss, don't you?"

Jerking her head sideways, she stared up at her maid. "Why do you call him that?"

Betsey shrugged. "It just seems fittin', is all."

"He's not your boss, you know."

She harrumphed again. "Ain't nobody 'cept'n you be my boss—you and the good Lord and maybe Woodson. Sometimes."

Carina chuckled. "It's good you included your husband, although you and I both know he's not the boss of the family."

Betsey gave her a stern look. "Now don't you be tellin' him that. What he don't know won't hurt him."

Laying her head back against the rocker, Carina smiled. She hadn't smiled since Dr. Bishop left two days ago. She hoped he didn't come back. It would be the easiest thing for them both—and for her heart, for she feared he'd unwittingly staked a claim on it. But that could never be. Her fader would never allow it.

"What's got you so down in the dumps?"

Carina twisted her mouth up to one side, unsure how much to tell Betsey. Her maid was the only person she could really talk to, other than Abel, and there were only certain things they could discuss. Susan had started coming around more often, though, but she could hardly talk to the doctor's mother about him.

"Go on and admit it. You miss him, too."

"Who?"

Betsey gave Carina's chair a shove, setting it into motion. "You know who."

She shook her head. "It could never work. Fader would never allow it."

"Yo' daddy ain't gonna be alive forever, now is he? You best be considerin' the future before you find it arrived and done left you behind."

Some days it seemed as if her fader would live forever. He was too cranky to die. She winced at the sliver of guilt that pricked her for even thinking such a thing. "How is he? I haven't seen him since the accident." She had no desire to see him.

"That weren't no accident. He threw that bottle on purpose, and you know it."

"I shouldn't have stood up to him. He doesn't like people doing that."

"He don't like much of anythin', if'n you ask me."

"Don't be mean."

Betsey pulled over the other rocker and sat down. "Yo' daddy is the mean one. He needs to find God, just like you do. I keep tellin' you that you don't have to bear all yo' burdens alone. God can he'p."

Carina closed her eyes, dreading another lecture about God. "Why would He help me now, when He's never done it before?"

"Hmpf. You don't know what He done and what He ain't done. How do you know He ain't already he'ped you?"

Carina jumped up. Was it too much to hope for a little peace and quiet on her own front porch? "He didn't help when Mother died, and He didn't save Johan."

"Yo' mama, she had a weak heart, child. And it's a blessin' that she didn't have to live all these years with yo' daddy, him being a mean ol' curmudgeon and all."

Pacing to the end of the porch, she saw Woodson walking up the road with another man, one who was leading a horse. Her heart jumped, and she narrowed her gaze. Could Reed have returned already?

" 'Tain't the doctah. His shoulders is too big."

Disappointment pressed down on her in spite of her decision to avoid Reed Bishop. "I wonder who it is."

"Don't know. I'd best get these peas a-cookin'. I'll check back in a few minutes, in case you want tea or coffee for yo' guest."

"He's not my guest."

"Well, he sure ain't come to see me." The door banged again.

Carina smiled at her maid's sassiness. Though it didn't always sound like it, Betsey respected her—she knew that. Carina actually enjoyed her maid's cheekiness and how it livened up her monotonous life. She watched the two men. The fact that the white man walked side by side with Woodson spoke volumes about him. So many white men forced their slaves to lag behind them.

They drew up to the porch, and the stranger removed his hat and smiled. "Ma'am, I'm William Dean. I bought the farm about four miles down the road. Used to be the Marshal place."

Carina nodded a greeting, thankful that Woodson did not leave her alone with Mr. Dean. Was he just being neighborly—whatever that was—or was there something he wanted? Should she ask him to sit? She tightened her hands on the porch rail. For a woman who lived in the South, her social skills were terribly lacking. "Nice to meet you, Mr. Dean. I'm Carina Zimmer."

Laugh lines crinkled in the corners of his brown eyes. His straw-colored hair hung thick and a bit shaggy. Betsey was correct about his shoulders being wider than the doctor's, although they were nowhere near as inviting to cry on. She ground her back teeth together. *Stop thinking about him.*

"How can I help you, Mr. Dean?"

He glanced at Woodson, then down at the ground. Carina glanced past her visitor to her servant. "Maybe you could water Mr. Dean's horse for him?"

Woodson gave a brief nod. She knew he understood her desire for him to stay close enough to keep an eye on things but far enough away to give them some privacy.

"That would be nice. Thank you." Mr. Dean handed off the reins.

"Would you care for some refreshment?"

He glanced at the front door then back at her. "If it wouldn't be too much trouble, ma'am. I could use a drink of water. That smoke kind of sticks to your throat after a while."

She invited him to have a seat then stuck her head in the doorway and called for Etta. After a long moment, the girl sashayed toward her. "Etta, I have a guest. Could you please bring us some tea, a glass of water, and some of your mama's shortbread?"

The girl's eyes went wide, but she nodded. "Yes'm."

Having guests was a rare occasion at Tanglewood, and she suspected both Etta and her mother would be listening near the door before too long. Stepping back outside, she reclaimed the rocker on the opposite side of the porch, leaving a more than respectable distance between her and Mr. Dean.

His gaze shifted toward the house, and Carina's eyes followed. She grimaced, realizing for the first time in a long while how sad her home must look to others. The place needed a fresh coat of milk paint, but when was she supposed to find the time for that?

"I moved here from Virginia a few months back," he said, curling the brim of his worn planter's hat. "Abigail Marshal was my great-aunt. She didn't have children, so when she died, she left the place to me."

Carina nodded, not sure why he was confessing all this to her.

A soft smile tilted his lips. "I've got me the most darling two young'uns you've ever laid eyes on. Clifton is five, and Lucy is just three. She's got her mama's blue eyes." A crease darkened his brow, as if his comment disturbed him for some reason.

Blue eyes—that put her in mind of a certain man she was trying hard to forget. She guided her thoughts in a different direction, trying to think of something neighborly to say. "We also moved here from the North when I was a girl. How is your wife adapting to living in the South?"

He frowned, making Carina wonder what she'd said that bothered him. Maybe his wife didn't like it here. Footsteps sounded, and Betsey carried a heavily laden tray outside, her gaze shifting straight to Mr. Dean. She set the tray down on a small table on the far side of his chair. Carina blew out a breath, hoping her maid would be nosy and stay close. And if she was going to be a proper hostess, she probably should move close enough that she could actually reach the tea. She rose, and Mr. Dean shot to his feet so fast that Betsey gasped and jumped back clear against the porch railing, her eyes wide and her hand on her heart.

Carina couldn't help the giggle that slipped out. She rarely saw her maid move so fast.

Mr. Dean's ears turned beet red. "Sorry for frightening you, ma'am."

Betsey's surprise at the apology addressed directly to her was obvious probably only to Carina. "No never mind. Have a seat, sir, and I'll po' you some tea." She cast a confused glance at Carina.

"I was just going to change chairs, so that I could serve the tea."

Betsey hiked her chin. "I do the servin' here. You just sit back down and talk to yo' guest."

If Mr. Dean thought her maid's bossiness odd, he didn't reveal it in his expression. He waited for her to sit then did so himself. Nice as he was, she was ready for this visit to be over. Having him here somehow seemed a betrayal of Dr. Bishop, not that that made a bit of sense to her. She looked across the yard to see if Woodson had finished watering Mr. Dean's horse.

Betsey handed Mr. Dean a glass of water, then poured the tea into cups. She added a spoon of sugar and a few drops of cream, just as Carina preferred it, and carried it to her. Blocking her guest's view with her body, her maid's brows lifted then waggled up and down. Carina waved a hand of dismissal, hoping Mr. Dean didn't notice. Betsey merely wandered back to the far side of the table. "What would you like in yo' tea, sir?"

"Oh, uh. . .just sugar." His gaze swiveled back to Carina. "Um. . .you asked about my wife, ma'am." His lips pressed into a thin line. "She passed on just over a year ago."

"Oh, I'm sorry." Carina didn't know what else to say. She had no experience in friendly conversation and had already made one faux pas.

He shook his head and smiled. "It's all right. You had no way of knowing." His gaze darted to Betsey then back to Carina. He set the glass down and leaned toward her. "I know this is going to sound rash, but I came here with a purpose, Miss Zimmer. You have a. . ." His gaze darted around the yard. "Uh. . .a fine plantation, ma'am."

Carina tried hard to ignore his phony use of *fine*, found it difficult. Did he think she'd sell him her land? Didn't he say he just got a farm?

He ran his hand through his thick hair and stood, paced past her to the end of the porch, then turned. "I don't need more land, Miss Zimmer. I'm a widower—a widower who desperately needs a wife."

fourteen

Reed's gaze traveled down Market Street, taking in the changes since he was last in town. "I was so anxious to get back to Reed Springs—to be home and to see Mother when I first returned from Scotland—that I didn't even notice the changes here."

Damian nodded. "New buildings shoot up around here faster than storms blow in off the sea." He snapped his fingers. "Oh hey, the city has plans to build a new customs house straight up ahead on the other side of East Bay Street."

Reed looked down the long street to the far end where East Bay Street intersected it. "Isn't that mostly marshland?"

"At the moment. They plan to fill it in."

Shaking his head, Reed said, "It's amazing what men can do when they put their heads together."

Damian clapped Reed's shoulder. "Speaking of what men can do, congratulations on becoming a doctor."

"Thank you. I can't say I enjoyed every minute of my studies and working long hours at the infirmary, but learning so much about the human anatomy, how to aid it in healing, and how to mend lacerations and fractured bones. . .well, it was fascinating."

Grinning, Damian shook his head. "You always did like tending injured animals."

"True, and remember that time you cut your arm and wouldn't let your mother care for it?"

"Right. I wanted my good friend Dr. Reed to see to my wounds."

Reed chuckled. "You're fortunate you didn't die from a blood disease."

Both men stepped to the side, tipped their hats, and allowed a trio of women to pass by, then resumed walking side by side. Street vendors hawked their wares, pedestrians walked along the other side of the street, some casually strolling, others striding with purpose. He loved coming to Charleston, partaking of all it had to offer, but his home was Reed Springs, and until this very moment, Reed had never realized the truth of that.

"You can't imagine my surprise to look up from my desk and see you standing in my office. I didn't even realize you had returned."

"Did you not get my last letter?"

Damian harrumphed. "Which letter would that be? The one I got in 1849 or the one in 1851?"

Reed felt his ears grow warm. "I was very busy, and besides, I don't remember receiving more than a handful of letters from you, either." He nudged his friend with his elbow. "Whatever happened between you and that gal you wrote me about who you met on that trip to Boston? What was her name? Melanie?"

Holding up his index finger, Damian waited while a carriage of giggling young girls drove past them. "*Melody*, and she's sweet music to my soul."

Rolling his eyes, Reed said, "And you once accused me of waxing poetic, if I remember correctly."

His friend slowed his pace then turned in the open door of a café. "This is the place I was telling you about earlier."

Reed sniffed the fragrant air. Pastries were fresh from the oven if he wasn't mistaken. "If the food tastes as good as it smells, we're in for a treat."

"Trust me, my friend, it does. I eat here frequently."

They took a table near the front window, which allowed Reed to watch the people coming and going. Charleston was so different from Glasgow. He studied the café, from its tall walls of dark wood to its small tables. "So, what's tasty here?"

"I like their chicken and dumplings."

"Sounds good to me. What happened between you and this Melody?"

Damian had always smiled more than anyone Reed had ever met, but the smile that revealed his somewhat crooked teeth now was the biggest one he'd seen on his friend.

Reed lifted his brows. "Good news, from the looks of it."

Damian clapped Reed on the forearm and leaned toward him. "I know you'll find this hard to believe, considering the frisky colt I used to be, but I'm now a happily married man."

Reed's mouth dropped open, and he stared at his friend, hardly able to believe what he was hearing. *Damian* and *marriage* were not two words he'd ever have used together in a sentence.

Chuckling, his friend shook his head. "I knew the news would bamboozle you. But there's more."

Reed blinked. "How can there be more? You have two wives?"

A young woman stopped at their table and rattled off the list of items available. Damian ordered for them both while Reed sat back in his chair and studied his friend. There was definitely a maturity that hadn't been present before. Why, his old buddy didn't so much as wink at the winsome waitress.

When she walked away to wait on another table, Reed leaned forward. "What else is there?"

"I'm going to be a father come this summer."

Completely stymied, he fell back against his chair. "Uh. . . congratulations."

"Hey, hey." Damian chuckled. "That's about the same response I had." He tugged at his collar. "A bit hard to take it all in, isn't it?"

Reed nodded. "True, but you seem happy and more settled than I've ever seen."

"I am settled. Very happy and very settled. Can hardly believe I'm going to be a father, though. All that's a bit scary."

"You'll do fine, I'm sure."

Damian leaned toward him. "And you'll deliver the baby, right?"

All manner of thoughts assailed him—of the numerous women he'd seen die as a result of childbirth, of the infants who had died. The last thing he wanted was something like that to come between him and his best friend. "I. . .uh. . . am honored you'd want me, but I don't plan to practice in Charleston. There are plenty of doctors here already."

Scowling, Damian pursed his lips and stared out the window. "Where then? Will you move to a smaller town or travel out West?"

"No, I've just hired two men to build a clinic at Reed Springs, up near the main road. That way I can stay close to Mother."

"Ah, I see. She's still trying to get you to run the plantation, eh, and you're still trying to avoid it." His friend caught his eye. "Might be easier to steer clear if you don't live there."

The hum of conversation and clatter of forks against plates surrounded him, as he struggled to put his thoughts to words. "I'm not trying to steer clear of my responsibility. That's part of the reason I decided to settle there—so I can be near Mother and oversee things at Reed Springs and treat the people in the area. They need a doctor."

"I don't like the fact that you aren't going to be here to

deliver my child, but I see the wisdom in your choice. So, have you had any patients yet?"

He nodded, his thoughts shooting straight as a lead ball to Carina. Had she missed him? Or was she glad that he was no longer coming around? "Actually, yes. I splinted a man's fractured leg and sutured a woman's forehead." *A very beautiful, spirited woman.*

Damian crossed his arms on the table, leaning forward with an intense stare; then he pointed his index finger at Reed. "What's that look I just saw?"

"What look?"

"That goofy kind of grin that I saw in the mirror for the first few months after I fell in love."

How did one answer such a question? Was his attraction to Carina so obvious?

"What woman did you sew up? Was she unmarried?"

Reed did not want to have this conversation. Damian would take a tiny thread of information and run with it. "Just a neighbor. That's all."

Damian's eyes rolled up as if he were searching his mind, trying to remember all the people who lived near him. After a moment he looked at him again. "What woman?"

"No one in particular."

"Well, does she have a name?"

Reed nodded and watched a wagon loaded with feed sacks pass by. WOOSTER GRAINARY—with an *i*, rather than the correct spelling of *Granary*—had been painted on the side of the vehicle.

Damian cleared his throat. "Well? The more you draw this out, the more interested I'm getting. Must be a very special lady."

He glanced at his friend. "It was Carina Zimmer."

Scowling, Damian tapped the table. "Zimmer." Suddenly

his eyes widened. "Any relation to Johan Zimmer?"

Pursing his lips, Reed nodded. "His sister."

Damian fell back against his chair, looking stupefied. "Well, that certainly was unexpected. And how did that go?"

Reed sniffed a sarcastic laugh. "She sent me a letter, challenging me to a duel." He conveyed all that had happened, including his growing attraction to a woman who despised him. He needed to talk to another man, especially one who had gone through this whole falling-in-love-and-getting-married thing.

"Wow. That's some story, my friend."

"Yes, it is, but what should I do about her?"

Damian's brows lifted. "What do you *want* to do?"

"I don't know."

"I guess you need to figure that out. You mentioned in one of your letters that you became a believer in Christ. Have you prayed about your relationship with Miss Zimmer?" He waved his hand in the air. "I mean, with all that's gone on in your past, I'd think you'd need a word from God before pursuing her."

The waitress bustled over and set a basket of sliced bread in the center of the table. She hurried back to the counter then returned with two plates of steaming chicken and dumplings. While his friend was distracted with his food, Reed marveled at how wise he seemed to have grown—from a joking hooligan to a married man and soon-to-be father. And when had *God* become a word Damian was so comfortable with?

Picking up his fork, he stirred his food. He'd prayed about Carina, hadn't he? Yes, he was certain he had, but not nearly enough. He took a bite of dumplings, closing his eyes as he savored the salty dish. One thing was for certain, if I-never-take-anything-serious Damian could find a woman, get married, and be happy, so could he.

❧

Carina paced the hallway just outside her fader's door. She'd put off seeing him for as long as she dared. The last thing she wanted to do was to make him angry again. Taking a bolstering breath, she peered inside and found him sitting up in bed, staring out the window.

He noticed her and turned her way, frowning. His normal expression. "Well, what do you want? What have you sold off now? The back half of my house?"

His house. Not theirs, just his. She ducked her head, wondering why she even felt the need to come visit him. "I just. . .umm. . .thought I'd see if there was anything you needed."

"Hmpf. It's about time." He lifted his head, and his scowl deepened. "What's that thing on your head?"

She lifted her hand, touching the cloth tied around her forehead. "A bandage."

"Why? What did you do?"

Carina stared at him with disbelief. "You honestly don't remember?"

He shook his head.

"You walloped her with a bottle, that's what." Betsey bustled through the door, arms crossed over her bosom. Carina had been so worried about seeing her fader that she never even heard her maid's approach—and that wasn't something easy to miss.

"I did no such thing." He turned his fiery gaze toward Carina. "Why didn't you sell off that yappy woman instead of Amos? Why do you let her tell such lies against your own fader?"

Most of her life she'd been afraid of her fader, yet she'd wanted his approval. But Betsey had been the one to hold her when she fell down, to encourage her, to teach her right from wrong. Betsey had loved her when her own fader felt nothing but disdain. Carina lifted her head. If he threw another bottle at her, so be it. "Because it's the truth. You got angry and threw a bottle at me."

"Lies! Get out! Both of you. Out of my sight." He grabbed a pillow and pitched it at her.

Betsey hurried out the door. Carina caught the pillow and held it to her chest. She might have found the nerve to stand up to her fader, but his rejection still hurt. A parent shouldn't hate a child for no reason. "From now on, I'll have one of the men bring up your meals."

The look he shot her could have curdled fresh milk. "Get me another bottle of whiskey."

Carina walked over to the sofa and laid the pillow on it. This topic was bound to come up sooner or later, so it might as well be now while she was feeling so bold. "There isn't any left."

"What! Why not?"

"Because there's no money with which to purchase it."

He snatched up the empty bottle hidden among his quilts and hugged it. "Sell something else. A horse. A cow. Another slave."

"No, Fader. I will not sell something we need just to fuel your habit. You will have to learn to live without it, as I have learned to do without so many things I need." She spun on her heel, unwilling to argue with him.

"Carina! Carina! You get back here!"

She hiked her skirts and hurried downstairs. If she could have done so with her ears covered, she would have.

"I'll sell that woman, you hear me, girl?"

Carina sniffed, trying valiantly to hold back her tears. She didn't want him to have the power to upset her. She needed to be stronger than him. When she reached the bottom stairs, Betsey was there. Carina fell into her big arms and was squashed against her maid's chest. Then the tears fell.

"It'll be all right, sweet child. Yo' Betsey is here."

"I'll never be able to please him."

"Nobody can, sweet thing. He's got a world of hurt all bottled up inside him, and it spews forth whenever an'body goes near him, just like a mad critter. It ain't no fault of yo's. That man, he needs the Lord Jesus in his heart."

She was so tired of being strong, of being the one in charge. She endured Betsey's jiggling, because next to being in Reed Bishop's arms, there was no place more comforting. "What would I do without you?"

"Hmpf. I don't know, child, but ol' Betsey, she ain't always gonna be here. That's why you gots to learn to take yo' burdens to the Lord. He be the only One who'll always be there for you."

Carina closed her eyes, too exhausted to argue. *Are you really there, God? If what Betsey says is true—that You'll always be there for me—show me. Show me that You're real. Somehow. Some way.*

fifteen

Carina guided Lulu around the far edge of the largest of her three crop fields. Her fader once grew tobacco here, but the rich soil was now divided into sections of turnips, peas, carrots, and brown potatoes, which waved their greenery in the warm breeze as if greeting her. Soon she would need to plant sweet potatoes and okra. She hadn't yet decided if she'd made a mistake to switch crops and grow vegetables, but she couldn't abide smoking and had quickly grown uncomfortable supporting selling tobacco, even though there was money to be made in such a crop. A smile tugged at her lips as she remembered something her mother had said: "If God had wanted people to smoke, He would have made their nose turn up like a smokestack."

That statement always set her fader off on a tirade of how her mother didn't appreciate all his hard work to put food on the table and a roof over their heads. Carina never understood that argument, because it was their slaves who labored, not him. He merely told the overseer what to do, as far as she'd been able to tell; then he'd visit in his study with friends, drinking, smoking, and playing games of chance. Her mother had never succeeded in getting him to stop smoking in the house, but at least Carina had. That was one thing she was proud of. When he first became bedridden, he'd fallen asleep smoking one night, and if she hadn't checked on him as she was heading to bed, the whole house might have burned down instead of just the quilt being damaged. After that she'd

131

refused to buy him cigars, and he was forced to quit smoking. Now that she'd refused to buy him liquor, would he become even more difficult to live with?

She rubbed her eyes and yawned. Several times through the night, she'd woken up to the crackling of glass breaking—a drinking glass or a vase he'd thrown against the wall—and to his cries for liquor to ease his pain. Was she wrong to refuse him? Was he in real pain, or was that just an excuse to get his way?

Sometimes she felt as if she were the parent and he the child.

She made a clicking sound and tapped her heels against Lulu's back, and the mare started walking again. Her injured leg had healed well and no longer seemed to bother her, but for now, Carina would keep her to a slow gait. She adjusted the skirt of her only dress to hide the calf that peeked out from under her petticoat, a dress that had extra-full skirts that allowed her to ride astride and still keep her legs from showing.

The rapid *tap-tap-tap* of a woodpecker echoed across the open field, providing a sharp contrast to the slower *whacks* of Chester's ax as he chopped firewood for Betsey's stove. The early morning fog had burned off, revealing a clear sky almost as brilliant as Dr. Bishop's eyes. She circled around the far side of the field, checking for weeds and dryness, then crossed over the ditch that connected to the Ashley River—a ditch her fader had ordered dug years ago to make watering the fields easier. One of the wisest decisions he'd ever made.

Woodson and Enoch were crouched down, plucking weeds from around tiny melon sprouts. Her mouth watered at the thought of the juicy fruit that always tasted refreshing on a hot day. Woodson stood and sauntered toward her. She reined Lulu to a stop and waited.

"Seedlin's is lookin' good."

She nodded. "Yes, they are. I'm sure hoping for a nice crop this year."

He nodded. "I'm askin' the good Lord for His blessing on your land, too."

"Thank you. That's kind of you."

The tall, thin man shook his head. "No, Miz 'Rina, it's a selfish prayer. I likes to eat as good as any person, and my Betsey, she needs plenty of them good vege'bles to keep her happy and cookin' up a storm." He grinned and winked at her.

Carina chuckled. "That's true, but I do thank you anyway." She nodded to the left. "Speaking of vegetables, looks like some of our greens are ready to be picked. Can you get to that before lunch, so I can let Betsey know to expect them?"

"Yes'm, we can do that. I'd best get back to work, or Enoch'll get ahead of me. We's racin' to see who can weed our section the fastest."

"Go on then." She smiled her thanks, and he nodded, then ambled back to where he had been working. Woodson never seemed in a hurry, but he was a hard worker and managed to keep the other men productive. She was blessed to have such loyal people working for her.

Blessed. That wasn't a word she'd often used. Her life had been so hard. Was it true, as Betsey had said, that her burdens would be lighter if she had faith in God? She tilted her head back, lifted the brim of her sun hat, and gazed up at the sky. *Are You truly up there, God?*

No answer came, but her thoughts turned to a scripture she'd read in her mother's Bible the night before. Something about God blessing her land if she humbled herself and prayed.

Betsey had told her many times that she should open her heart to her heavenly Fader. To trust Him and rely on Him to lighten her burdens. That He was a Fader of love, patience, and peace.

But she'd never had a loving fader. Wouldn't even know what one was if not for watching Woodson with Sammy and Etta all these years. He was firm but playful. Teaching and patient. He hugged them. Teased them. Loved them.

She was jealous of a slave.

And yet those slaves were her true family. They cared for her.

Her gaze lifted to the sky. She wanted to believe there was a greater power at work in the world. One who cared about people. One who cared about her. "Help me, God. Show me that You are real."

⁓

Carina rode into the yard and discovered a buggy near the paddock. A pair of feet hung over the backseat—the napping driver, she suspected. Her gaze shot to the house then down at her old work dress. She swiped her eyes, damp from tears that had come as she beseeched God to help her.

Sammy left Chester's side, where he'd been stacking wood, and raced toward her. "Mama says to tell you that Mizzes Bishop be here and fo' you to get on inside in a hurry."

She slid to the ground and tossed him Lulu's reins. No need to tell him to take care of her beloved horse. Untying her bonnet, she hurried around to the far side of the house and peeked into the kitchen that set back a hundred feet or so from the main building. Stomach-teasing odors emanated from the room, but her maid was not there. Etta sat on a stool on the far side of Betsey's worktable, staring off into space. "Where's your mama?"

The girl jumped and snatched up the sampler she'd been working on for as long as Carina could remember. "You scared the wits out of me, Miz 'Rina. Made me mess up my stitchin'."

Pursing her lips, Carina resisted shaking her head. "Where's Betsey?"

"In the parlor, seein' to Mizzes Bishop. That Doctah Boss's mama is real nice."

She nodded her agreement then jogged to the back door, hung up her hat, and gazed in the mirror of the hall tree. Her cheeks were red and her unruly hair damp and curling in all the wrong directions. She licked her hands and attempted to smooth it down, but to no avail. Would it be terribly rude to just wear her hat in the house? No, Betsey would never let her get away with that.

With a deep sigh, she hurried to the parlor, stopping just outside the entrance. Susan Bishop sat on the sofa, sipping tea and talking to Betsey. Carina's heart flip-flopped. Had the doctor come with his mother? Abel had made no mention of him when she stopped to visit with him a few minutes ago. She leaned forward just enough to see that he wasn't in the room. Disappointment warred with relief. She didn't know what to say to him when she next saw him, and she knew she would before too long. Her hand lifted to the sutures in her forehead. Would it hurt when he removed them?

"The candy is quite tasty. Hard—made of cooked molasses, brown sugar, and butter that is boiled for a half hour or so. Then you add a quart of parched and shelled groundnuts, pour the mixture in a shallow tin, and allow it to cool, so my friend from up north in Baltimore said. You break off a piece small enough to fit easily in your mouth," Susan said. "So tasty. Oh, and imagine this. . .she found the recipe in *The Carolina Housewife*. Isn't that ironic."

Betsey nodded, looking mesmerized, although Carina wondered if she knew what *ironic* meant. It was little wonder Susan's son had no qualms about treating a black man, when his mother, the epitome of a plantation mistress, didn't mind conversing with a slave and even treated her as an equal.

"That sounds mighty fine. Bet my Sammy and Miz 'Rina would like that." Betsey glanced past Susan, noticed Carina, and stood. "Speakin' of her, here she be."

Susan's warm smile helped settle Carina's unease. "What a pleasure to have you visit again." Carina took the seat Betsey had vacated, her mind begging to ask about Reed. Was he back from Charleston? Did he find the horse he wanted? Did he think about her while he was gone?

"How is your head doing, dear? Does it still pain you?"

She shook her head. "No, ma'am. Not so much." Carina glanced down, noticing the dirt under her fingernails from when she'd walked the fields and plucked some weeds earlier. She slipped them under the folds of her skirt, which now seemed ridiculously abundant, hoping Susan wouldn't notice. Reed's mother always appeared perfect. Her hair was immaculate, in spite of the fact she'd ridden over in the buggy. Her dress, a beautiful royal blue and light blue, didn't so much as have a wrinkle. Why, she doubted the woman ever sweated. "And. . .um. . .how have you been?"

"Perfectly fine, thank you. Especially now that Reed is back."

Carina realized too late that she'd reacted to the mention of the doctor, and there was little doubt Susan had noticed. Her lips turned up in a gentle smile; her brown eyes twinkled.

"I'm hoping he will come and remove these sutures. They pinch at times."

Susan's smile dimmed. "I'm sure he will. He's just a bit distracted at the moment. The men he hired to build his clinic returned from Charleston with him, and they are at this very moment laying the foundation. Reed was there watching when I passed by on my way here. His enthusiasm is as contagious as the plague."

She couldn't help smiling, just imagining him out there planning where to put his surgical table, how he'd arrange his medicines and his instruments. He was a good doctor, caring and gentle.

Susan cocked her head. "You like him, don't you, dear?"

She lifted her hands to her warm cheeks, knowing they gave her away. "I. . .uh. . ."

"It's all right. I didn't mean to embarrass you."

Susan's hopeful smile sent prickles of guilt racing down Carina's spine. She leaned forward, clasping her hands together. "Please don't misunderstand me. I do like your son, but there can be nothing between us other than friendship. My fader would never allow it."

"Fathers have a way of changing their minds when it comes to their daughters. Mine was completely opposed to my marrying Frank at first. I think it's because he knew we'd be spending so much time out at the plantation, and he would miss me. But it all worked out."

Carina shook her head. "My fader will never yield. In fact, if he knows I want something, he's even more adamant against it." The truth of the matter hurt her deep within. Susan had a father who loved her so much he didn't want to lose her. She blinked back tears.

"What's wrong, dear? I'm sorry if I upset you." Susan stood and rushed to her side, resting her hand on Carina's shoulder. "Tell me, dear. What is it?"

She pressed her lips together and shook her head. Even though she longed to share her doubts, to explain how her father mistreated her, what would it accomplish? Nobody could understand. "I would have to speak ill of my fader to explain it."

Susan squatted down and caught Carina's gaze. "It's admirable that you don't want to talk about him, but sometimes it does a soul good to share your problems with another person. It doesn't have to be me, but I do encourage you to find someone you're comfortable talking with. I've found that it helps ease your burden." She pushed on the armrests and slowly stood. "Oh, my knees aren't as flexible as they used to be."

Carina jumped up to steady her. "Are you all right?"

"I'm fine, but I do believe I'll be applying some of that liniment my son prescribed when I return home. I took a fall down the stairs once when I was younger and twisted my left knee. It's never been quite the same."

"I'm relieved to know you have a flaw." Carina gasped and covered her mouth. "Oh my. That didn't come out quite right."

Susan's shoulders jiggled; then she laughed aloud. "I'm far from flawless. Just ask my son."

Smiling back, she tried to relax, grateful that Susan was not as quick to take up an offense as her fader was.

"Would you mind if we walked a bit? I tend to get stiff if I sit too long."

"Of course not." Carina held out her palm. "After you."

Susan stopped at the front door and donned her lovely bonnet. Carina had rarely ever seen one quite so fancy with its lace and ribbons. She decided to leave her ragged straw hat hanging.

Betsey entered the back door and hurried toward them. "You ain't leavin' already? I was hopin' Miz 'Rina might invite you to stay fo' lunch."

If Susan was repulsed by the maid's impertinence in offering an invitation instead of Carina, she didn't show it. "Why, thank you so much. I would love to stay sometime, but Reed is expecting me home in time to dine with him. If I don't return on time, he's likely to come looking for me." She laid her fingertip across her lips, eyes gleaming. "Then again, maybe I should stay."

Was Reed Bishop's mother playing matchmaker? Surely Carina had mistaken her meaning. Why would she possibly encourage a union of her highly sought-after son with a woman who had so little to offer?

Chuckling, Susan laid her hand on Carina's forearm. "I'm only teasing, dear. Don't get in a panic."

"Miz 'Rina can send you an invitation to come next week, and maybe you can bring Doctah Boss with you." Betsey lifted her chin slightly, as if not yet ready to concede defeat.

Widening her eyes, Carina shot her a glance, urging her to hush. It was a good thing she didn't have company very often, because she'd probably be in a constant state of embarrassment.

"I'd like that, and I'm sure Reed would, too."

Carina couldn't help wondering if the two women were in cahoots with each other. Maybe she'd just let Susan and Betsey dine with the doctor while she made herself scarce.

"Oh, before I forget, I need to give you something." Susan reached for her handbag that lay on the hall-tree bench, opened it, and pulled out a cream-colored paper that had been rolled up like a scroll and tied with a lavender ribbon. "This is for you."

Her mouth went dry as she reached for the paper. What could Susan have needed to write her that couldn't be spoken face-to-face? Her index finger slid over the embossed stationer's mark that indicated the fine quality of the paper.

"Go ahead. Open it," Susan prodded.

She glanced at Betsey, who nodded her eager encouragement. With dread, Carina untied the ribbon and unrolled the paper to reveal a fancy script:

To Miss Carina Zimmer,

Mrs. Frank R. Bishop requests the honour of your presence at a ball to be given in honour of her son's return home and his achievement as a surgeon.

Carina couldn't read any further. A ball. She hadn't been to a ball since. . .

"Now don't start fretting, dear." Susan offered a heartening smile. "I realize that you haven't been to many social events of late, but where better to start than my home? You won't have far to travel, and it will give you the chance to personally thank your neighbors who did such a lovely job on your drive."

Carina glanced at Betsey, who lifted her brows, her eyes wide, and eagerly nodded. No help there.

How could she face all those people? She had nothing to wear. She couldn't possibly agree, no matter how much it might disappoint Susan. "I—"

A thump sounded on the porch, then the front door flew open. Sammy burst in, eyes wide and tears streaming down his cheeks. He grasped hold of her skirt and gazed up at her. "Miz 'Rina! Some man done took Lulu!"

sixteen

Reed walked the foundation of his clinic. Would the four-room structure be large enough? He'd have a room where family members could wait, a private examination room that could double as his surgical room, and two separate areas for male and female patients. He stood with his hands on his hips and glanced heavenward. "Well, Lord, what do You think?"

One of the workers looked up. "Pardon?"

"Oh, nothing." Reed waved his hand in the air. They must think him odd, but he was sure they wouldn't mention it if they did.

The sound of pounding hoofbeats drew his attention to the road. His mother's buggy careened toward the side of the road, straightened, then began to slow. Reed ran toward it. Where was his mother? Had something happened to her?

Charlie jumped from the seat the moment the buggy stopped and met him. "Yo' mama sent me. There's been a theft at the Zimmers'. A horse and some food."

"Is Mother still there? Was anyone hurt?" *Is Carina all right?* he wanted to ask.

"Everyone's fine. Mrs. Bishop's the one that sent me. Says for you to get some men and ride the line between here and Tanglewood. It was a skinny white man that done the stealin'."

Reed's jaw clenched. It had to be the same man who had stolen food last week when they worked on the drive. He nodded his thanks. "Go back to the Zimmers' and stay there with Mother until I get there. I don't want her on the road if there's a dangerous man about. Tell Miss Zimmer I said it would be a good idea to arm herself and her workers."

Charley nodded. "Chester is stayin' 'round the house. Them other two men is followin' the tracks."

Reed hurried to Caesar and mounted. He wished now that he'd taken time to search for a better horse, but since the carpenters had been available, he'd been anxious to get back so they could get started. He galloped Caesar to the house, ran inside, and retrieved his Sharps rifle from his gun cabinet in the study.

Jarrod crept into the room with a fireplace poker in hand. "When I saw the door left open, sir, I thought we had an intruder."

"Ironic you should mention that. There's been another theft at the Zimmers', and word is he's headed this way. I'm headed out to search for him. Please alert some of our men to help with the search, and pass the word for the women and children to gather in a safe place."

Jarrod nodded. "Right away, sir."

Reed rushed outside and mounted. He prayed that the Lord would help him find the thief and that he would not get injured. A doctor needed to be healthy to take care of others.

Thuds from the horse's hooves echoed below the new bridge that had recently been built over the creek that paralleled their drive for a short way. The old gazebo needed replacing soon, too. Maybe that could be next on the carpenter's list. He rode past the pasture that held several dozen, fine-quality brood mares with newborn foals. How odd it was that the thief chose to steal one of the Zimmers' few horses when Reed Springs had an abundance of them. Maybe the thief avoided his place because of the numerous workers.

For close to an hour, he searched the acres of farmland, the groves of trees that hugged the river, and the woodlands that remained unused. He hadn't yet spotted either of Carina's men, and he'd almost reached the border between his land and hers. Slowing the horse, he listened for the sound of humans. Nothing but nature's chorus met his ears. The thrum of insects. A hawk screeching high overhead. Squirrels chattering in a nearby tree. A horse's whinny off in the distance.

Caesar lifted his head and pricked his ears forward, looking off to the right. Reed stared in the same direction. Had the animal heard something, or was he just listening for the other horse to whinny again? Could that have been Lulu?

A loud cry echoed through the trees. His horse pawed the ground and whickered. Something wasn't quite right, and Caesar sensed it. Reed turned him toward the noise, keeping his rifle ready. The horse plodded forward. Reed kept his ears attuned to the sounds around him, listening hard for anything out of the ordinary.

A short while later, he rode down a hill, and something white flapping in the trees across the field caught his eye. A woman's petticoat?

He reined Caesar around to the right, using the underskirt for cover. About fifty feet away, he slid out of the saddle. A shrill, catlike squeal halted his steps, and he lifted his rifle in case he needed it as his gaze searched the trees. Caesar jerked his head up and shied sideways, then trotted off. Reed lunged at him but missed. He spun back around. The petticoat lay on the ground, and he stood facing the thief he'd chased the week before—a thief who now held a gun on him.

"No! Don't shoot!" A woman who sat on the ground leaning back against a tree held up her palm toward Reed, then just as quickly lowered it to her swollen abdomen. "Oh, help me, Johnny."

The man glanced over his shoulder, his indecision obvious. Reed took a chance and lowered his rifle. He couldn't risk shooting with the woman lying so close to the man. If the thief shot him, so be it. "I'm a doctor. I can help."

The thief eyed him as if weighing his measure then nodded and tossed his gun to the ground. "Isn't loaded anyway."

Reed hurried to the woman's side and squatted. "Are you having birth pains, ma'am, or some other ache?"

She rolled her green eyes. "How should I know? This is my first baby."

He reached for her arm then paused. "May I?"

She frowned. Sweat beaded on her forehead, and her auburn hair hung damp. "May you what? Are you a real doctor?"

Reed smiled, hoping to reassure her. "May I take your pulse? And yes, I'm a real doctor—a surgeon, actually."

"What's a pulse? And I don't want no cuttin' on me." Her gaze lifted behind. "Johnny?"

The thief lowered himself to the ground beside the woman and took her hand. Reed glanced at him, noticing immediately how thin he was up close. "Are you ill?"

Johnny shook his head and looked away.

"He don't eat enough," the woman said. "He's been giving me most of the food because of the baby."

Reed's opinion of the man elevated somewhat, although thievery was never the answer for not having something to eat. Johnny looked to be close to his own age, and though about the same height, he was about half of Reed's weight.

"Oh, oh! The pain's comin' again. Help me."

She reached out to Reed. He grasped her wrist and checked her pulse, relieved to find it strong. Though on the thin side also, she didn't have sunken eyes and hollow cheeks like Johnny. He took her hand and waited for her pains to subside, and when they did, she let go of him, laid her head against the tree, and closed her eyes. "What's your name, ma'am?"

"Millie. Millie Jones."

"My name is Dr. Bishop."

Johnny's dull eyes popped open, and he stared at Reed. His shaggy beard touched his chest and held pieces of grass on one side as if he'd slept on the ground.

"We need to get your wife out of these woods. Can you take my rifle off a ways and fire it into the sky? There are other men nearby who can help us."

Johnny didn't move but glanced from Reed to Millie. In light of the fact he'd sacrificed the little food he had for his wife, Reed doubted the man would run off. So why the hesitation?

"Look," Reed said, "I know you're the man who took that food last week, and I'm guessing you are also the thief who stole food and a horse from Tanglewood today, but none of that matters now. You're about to be a father. Do you want your child born out here in the woods?"

He pursed his lips, lowered his gaze, and shook his head. Finally he rose and trudged to the rifle. Millie yelped when he fired into the air.

❧

"Do you see anyone yet?" Carina called to Sammy, who stood in the open window of the barn loft.

"Not yet." The boy shook his head.

"Be careful up there. We don't want you breaking your leg like Abel." Sighing, Carina walked back to the porch where Susan sat in one of the rockers, mending a pair of Sammy's pants. "What do you think is taking so long?"

"Maybe they had trouble getting the buggy through the trees. Didn't Enoch say Reed found that couple in the woods?"

"Yes. Do you think I should check the room again?"

Susan smiled. "I doubt anything's changed since you last checked it."

"I don't suppose so." Carina sat on the top step and rested her cheeks in her hands. She wasn't sure if she was more nervous about housing strangers in her home or seeing Reed again. What would she say to him? Would he still look at her with those beautiful eyes as if she were someone special? No one had ever looked at her like that, except maybe her mother, but she had died so long ago Carina could barely remember her.

Why hadn't Reed taken the couple to his home? It would be far quieter there, and the couple wouldn't have to endure her father's curses, moans, and retching. But then again, maybe that would work in her favor, and they wouldn't stay long. She twisted her hands together. What a gracious hostess she was.

"Stop your fretting, dear. Everything will work out."

Carina nodded, hoping Susan was right. Closing her eyes, she muttered the prayer she'd started repeating several times a day. *Help me, Lord. Give me strength.*

"Hey! Someone's a-comin'!" Sammy bounced up and down, far too close to the window's edge.

She jumped up. "You scoot back, right now. You hear me?"

He did, and then she noticed he wasn't looking in the direction she'd expected, but rather down the drive. She walked away from the house and lifted her hand over her eyes.

Susan came off the porch and joined her. "I thought they'd come from the other direction."

"Me, too." A sour feeling settled in the pit of Carina's

stomach as the wagon drew nearer. "That's not your buggy."

"Why, isn't that Mr. Dean?" Susan asked. "Oh, and look, he has his children with him." She started forward toward the wagon.

Carina followed, knowing for certain Susan wouldn't be so happy when she learned about Mr. Dean's last visit.

❧

Reed exhaled a huge sigh when the Zimmers' kitchen and then the big house came into view. Mrs. Jones was going to deliver her child within the hour—he was as certain as one could be without examining her. Unlike Carina, who preferred to keep her problems to herself, his patient had moaned and groaned the whole way, grumbling about every bump and jiggle. Her poor husband had sat up front next to Woodson, who drove the vehicle. Johnny had been slouched down with his hat covering his face most of the way. Reed wasn't certain if his odd behavior was due to his sad state of health, to avoid acknowledging his wife's complaints, or just because he was relieved to have help for her. He'd stayed off to himself once Woodson and Enoch arrived, then had disappeared until they left to fetch the wagon, and returned with Lulu.

"Oh, is this buggy ever gonna stop? Just kill me now and get it over with."

Reed couldn't help chuckling. "I know you're uncomfortable, Mrs. Jones, but I'm not about to let you die. Not if I can help it."

"I just want this over."

He glanced at the buildings again. Just a few more minutes, then they could get her into the house and into a bed. "What do you plan to name the baby?"

"Depends on if it's a girl or boy."

"Uh. . .yes, I suppose it does. And what if it's a girl?"

Mary shook her head. "Johnny don't want no girl. Said his papa wasn't never partial to girls, neither. I reckon we'll call him after his papa, Johnny."

"Won't that be confusing?"

She shrugged then grimaced and latched onto Reed's arm so hard he wondered if he'd be able to use it if needed. "Oh. . . somebody help me."

The buggy pulled to a stop, and Reed jumped down. Johnny slid off, and his knees buckled. Reed grabbed him. "Whoa there, hang on."

Footsteps sounded behind him, and he glanced over his shoulder, expecting to see Carina, but Will Dean met his gaze. Reed paused. What was *he* doing here?

"Need some help, Doc?"

He didn't have time now to analyze the situation. "Can you help this man upstairs so he can lie down?"

Will nodded and took Johnny's arm, all but dragging him toward the porch. "Where should I put him?"

"Ask Miss Zimmer." Reed hated ordering the man to initiate conversation with Carina, but he had no choice.

"Follow me, Mr. Dean," she said.

Reed's gaze snapped to hers, met, and held, like a ship tethered to its dock. Then she slipped away into the house, with his mother following.

Woodson hopped down and stood beside Reed, waiting for orders. "Help me get Mrs. Jones inside."

A short while later, with Mrs. Jones more comfortable in bed and Johnny lying on a cot facing the wall, Reed relaxed just a hair. Betsey had recruited Woodson to lug up a pot of hot water, while Etta collected some cloths and towels for the birthing. Carina stood in the hall, staring at Millie Jones. He longed to talk to her but knew the infant's birth was imminent.

Footsteps sounded in the hall; then his mother stepped around Carina and looked at her. "I talked with Mr. Dean and invited him to come another day when things were less hectic."

He couldn't tell if that was good news to Carina or not. He remembered the man stating how he was looking for a wife and inquiring after her. Had they come to an agreement already?

"Ay-yi-yi! I'm dying, I tell you."

"Reed," his mother called in a tone that always grabbed his attention. "Tend to your patient."

How could he tell her that he felt too awkward with Carina standing there watching? And Mrs. Jones hardly needed a crowd. "Mother, could you assist me?"

"Certainly, son. Just tell me what to do." She crossed to his side.

Carina's wounded stare nearly tore his heart out.

"Mr. Jones is badly in need of something to eat. Would you mind seeing if Betsey could make some broth? I fear it's been so long since he's eaten well that he won't be able to tolerate much."

She nodded then disappeared down the hall.

Mrs. Jones's wails made even her husband jump, but he was either too tired or too scared to look up from his bed.

seventeen

He didn't want her there. He'd asked his mother to help him, not her. Carina's chin quivered.

She hurried past her fader's door. He was the last person she wanted to see.

"Carina! What is all that caterwauling?"

She stopped. Sighed. He had a right to know what was happening. *Give me strength, Lord.*

She spun around and entered his room, stopping just inside the door. "I'm sorry for the disturbance, Fader. Dr. Bishop found a woman who is about to give birth, and he brought her here."

He pushed up from his pillows, scowling. "Why here? Why didn't he take that noisy—"

"Fader!"

Puckering up like an old turnip, he glared at her, and she glared back. At least he didn't have any bottles to lob at her.

"Why didn't the doctor take that woman to his own house? Doesn't he know there's an invalid here trying to rest?"

"The woman is very close to delivering, and our place was much closer. I will shut your door if it's bothering you so much."

"Fine. But I want them gone first chance they get. We aren't running a hotel here, and we've had to sell off our slaves just to eat."

"Leased, Fader. They will be returned to us when the contract expires." She glanced around his room, checking it. Betsey or Etta must have opened his window because it had been closed earlier. The nightshirt he'd worn the past few days lay in a heap on the floor at the foot of the bed. How odd that someone would have left it there and not placed it in the laundry pile. "Well, I need to be going. Do you want anything else?"

"Just some peace and quiet." He crossed his arms, and she took a good look at him. He'd aged a lot lately. His hair was white, not the light blond it used to be, and his dark eyes looked dull. He'd lost weight. "And my whiskey."

"I'm sorry, but we're out, and I don't intend to buy any more." She backed out, pulling the door shut. As she walked down the stairs with Mrs. Jones's loud grunts following her, she realized that her fader hadn't been as mean as in the past. Maybe her prayers were finally working.

She thought about how Reed had chased her from the room. Well, maybe some of them were working.

❦

Reed stood at the top of the stairs and listened to Carina down below, rattling off a list of things that needed doing today: laundry, the meal items that needed fixing, how Etta was to stay upstairs and work just in case he needed something. Betsey confirmed she had the items for the meals, then Carina walked to the front of the house. He stepped back, not wanting her to see him, but she exited out the front door, never even casting a glance his way.

From the window on the landing, he watched her stride with purpose out to the barn, wearing an old dress with skirts big enough to hide a horse under. She entered the shadows and out of his view. He blew out a sigh.

"So, what are you going to do about her, son?"

He spun around. "Who? Is something wrong with Mrs. Jones?"

"For a surgeon, sometimes you're not too smart. I'm talking about Carina."

He swallowed hard and tried not to look surprised. His mother always was perceptive. "I don't know. It seems like whenever I try to get close to her, she backs away. I'm not sure she doesn't still despise me." Voicing the thought that had chased him all week hurt more than he expected.

"I don't believe that's true." She laid her hand on his arm. "She's had a rough life, son, still does for that matter. She doesn't know how to depend on anyone but herself."

"So, how do I get her to trust me? She doesn't believe that Johan started that duel. She blames me for his death, and rightly so."

Her lips turned up in a sympathetic smile. "Give her a little time. She's been reading the Bible, and I believe God is drawing her near."

"I'm afraid I don't have a whole lot of time, not with Mr. Dean coming around." Reed turned back and looked out the window. Carina rode out of the barn on Lulu's back—riding astride. His mouth fell open. Would that woman never cease to surprise him?

"My stars."

His mother chuckled. "Carina's not exactly representative of your average Southern woman, is she?"

Reed had to smile. "No, she is not. That's for certain."

"Who's that out there?" a deep voice called from the room across from the one the Joneses were staying in.

His mother lifted her brows. "I'll check on Mrs. Jones and the baby and leave that old bear to you."

"What would the good ladies of your society club think if they heard such talk, Mother?" Though he pretended to be astonished at her name-calling, Reed couldn't help chuckling.

His mother winked and lifted her index finger to her lips. "Shh. . ."

He faced the door, steeling himself for the lambasting he knew was coming, and peered in. "It is I, Dr. Bishop. May I come in, sir?"

"What are you doing in my house again?"

"I delivered a baby last night."

"Oh, yeah. Carina told me there was strangers staying here."

He lifted his chin, and as the light from the open window illuminated his face, Reed could see the severe yellow cast to his chin. He stepped closer, wanting to look at the man's eyes. "How long has your skin been so yellow?"

"What!" He raised his arm and slid back the sleeve and stared at his skin. "What do you mean? Looks fine to me."

"Hmm. . .look at me, please." When he lifted his head with a haughty glower, Reed lifted one of the man's eyelids, unhappy to see the yellowing there also. "May I see your tongue?"

Mr. Zimmer surprised Reed by complying. "You're thinner than when I last saw you. How's your appetite?"

He fell back against his pillows as if just that small effort exhausted him. "Don't have one."

Reed had seen a number of patients at the infirmary in Glasgow with the same symptoms, and not a one of them got better. This was not news that Carina needed to hear. She already had far too many burdens on her thin shoulders already.

"Say, can you get me some liquor? This ache in my gut hurts me something fierce." He crossed his arms over his thin chest. "That closefisted daughter of mine refuses to buy me any."

"I'm afraid I can't do that, sir. That's between you and your daughter."

Mr. Zimmer's head snapped up. "You Bishops never did do

a thing to help a Zimmer. Get out of my room."

Reed moved off the side of the bed and stood. "I'm sorry you feel that way. I was hoping to talk to you about Carina."

"What about her?"

He hadn't planned out what to say if he ever got to talk to Carina's father. He still wasn't completely sure of his feelings—just that he had them—and they were strong. But God had opened an unexpected door, so he would step through. "I have feelings for her."

Karl Zimmer wrinkled up like a prune and muttered a curse. "Over my dead body. No Bishop will ever marry my daughter."

❧

Carina rushed up the steps. She'd forgotten her sun hat, which she'd left in her room yesterday. Her fader's harsh words gushed out the door, stabbing her heart. She'd been right. His animosity toward the Bishops was as strong today as ever. He would never allow her to marry Reed. She spun around, her heart breaking, and rushed down the stairs. She never should have gotten her hopes up.

eighteen

Carina held Millie's baby in her arms, watching the quiet little boy doze. Tufts of blond hair stuck up like duckling fuzz. "What did you name him?"

With her eyes never leaving her baby's face, she replied, "Jonathon Carl Jones."

"Karl?" Carina's gaze zipped to Millie's. "That's my fader's name. Will you spell it with a *C* or a *K*?"

One side of Millie's mouth cocked upward, and she shrugged. "I've only ever seen it spelled with a *C*."

"*K*. It's a *K*," Mr. Jones mumbled from the other side of the bed.

Carina and Millie looked at each other, brows lifted. Then they giggled. Millie's husband hadn't said a thing until that moment, as far as she knew.

"Come and see your son, Johnny. He's so sweet. He's got your nose, I believe."

"Not now. I'm tired."

Millie shrugged, but her disappointment was evident. Carina handed the baby back to his mother. "Will you call him Johnny like his father?"

"We haven't really talked much about that yet. I was thinking about maybe calling him J.J." She glanced over at her husband. "Is that all right, Johnny?"

He shrugged but didn't comment. The man was horribly thin. Susan had told her what Reed had conveyed to her— that he'd nearly starved himself to save his wife and baby.

Knowing the lengths he'd gone to—even stealing to keep them alive—had washed away any uncertainties she had about them staying with her. Maybe when Johnny got better, he'd be willing to help out around the plantation, and maybe she could find some way to pay him a small salary, though she had no idea how she'd do that.

"I'd best get back to work now. If you need anything, just holler."

Carina slipped down the hall into her room and shut the door. She pressed her skirts against her flat stomach. Would she ever marry? Would she ever know what it was like to carry a man's child? In that moment, as if someone had illuminated a dark room, she knew the truth. The only man's child she wished to carry was Reed's.

But that could never be.

◦•

Reed strode into the music room and dropped into a chair. His mother halted the song she was beautifully playing and smiled.

"The walls are up on two of the clinic's rooms already."

"So why aren't you happy?"

Reed shrugged. He knew, but he had yet to tell her.

She rose and glided toward him, perfectly presentable, even though the breakfast hour had barely passed. "Is it Carina?"

"I don't know what to do, Mother. I approached her father, but he said he would never approve a marriage between us."

She cocked one brow. "Marriage? You actually asked him that?"

Reed thought back a moment. "No, but I told him I had feelings for her."

"Hmm. . .the Bible does tell children to honor their fathers."

He opened his mouth to protest, but she held up her palm.

"Hear me out before you say anything." She took the chair next to his and turned toward him. "Give this over to the good Lord. If it's His will for you to marry Carina, trust Him to work it all out."

"You make it sound so simple."

"Well, frankly, it is. Either you trust God with your life and trust Him to help you through the problems in your life, or you don't."

Reed gave her a melancholy smile, for that was all his hurting heart could manufacture. "How did you get to be so wise?"

"Old age, I'm afraid. You'll be wise, too, once you start turning gray-headed."

"Some days I feel like I already am." He straightened in his chair, knowing what he had to say next would please her immensely. "I've been praying, Mother, and doing some thinking, and you're right."

"Wonderful! What am I right about?" Her brown eyes glimmered.

"About me and the plantation. I've realized that I need to step up and do my duty as part owner of Reed Springs. God showed me that I need to embrace my inheritance. After what happened at the duel, I felt I didn't deserve all of this. I wasted much of my youth, and being a surgeon, making my own way, was penance."

"Oh, Reed. All of this is a gift, just like God's love. You can never earn it, because it's already yours."

He smiled. "I know that now, Mother."

"Mama..."

He uttered a mock sigh and shook his head. "I'm happy to say, *Mama*, that as of today, you've been relieved of your duties."

"What duties?"

"All of them. Everything having to do with the plantation. I'm ready to take my place as planter—but I also intend to be a surgeon."

"Hmm. . ." She tapped her index finger against her lips. "Let me get this right. You plan to select all the meals for each day, and see that the maids dust behind the lamps, and oversee the spring cleaning and the hanging of netting on the beds?"

He sat back in his chair. "Uh. . .no. I'll leave those and the other household duties to you. How about this: anything inside you tend to, and outside duties will belong to me."

"That sounds wonderful, son." She hopped up. "Come with me."

He rose and followed. "Where are we going?"

"Outside."

He rolled his eyes at Jarrod as they passed him on their way out the back door. "Why are we going outside?"

"So I can show you how to hang up the laundry."

❧

If not for her heart breaking like an egg crushed under Woodson's big foot, everything else in Carina's life would have seemed as close to perfect as it could get. The crops were healthy and growing well. Her fader still grumbled but not so much as before when he'd been drinking. Baby J.J. and his mother were doing well, and she'd even seen Johnny outside at a distance, though the man seemed so shy that he wouldn't talk to anyone but his wife. At least he had Millie, and she seemed happy and contented.

She finished brushing Lulu and leaned her head against the mare's warm side. *Thank You, Lord, for giving her back to me.*

After giving her mare a final pat, she wandered back to the slave cabins to see Abel. She'd noticed him sitting outside under a tree when she rode back from checking the fields. He waved and flashed her that big, toothy grin she loved.

"Mornin', missy."

"Good morning, although it's getting closer to noon."

Abel pushed back his hat and looked up. "That it is. No wonder my belly's ticklin' my innards."

Carina chuckled. Abel had a way of making her laugh. "Would you like me to get something for you to eat?"

"Nah, I can wait a spell. Oh, oh!" He snatched up a long, narrow stick from off the ground and worked it down into the splint from the top side, then tugged it up and down. His eyes looked up, and a contented grin replaced his agitated look. "Ahh. . .that sure feels good. This ol' leg is about to itch off."

"Have you asked the doctor about that?" Just mentioning Reed made her miss him anew. She hung her head, wishing there was a way to change things.

"Ain't seen him since the day he delivered that baby. What was that—ten days or so?"

"Eleven."

"Not that nobody's countin'."

She glanced up but didn't smile, realizing she'd been doing exactly that. Pining for what she couldn't have was making her miserable.

"You needs to give yo' burden to the Lord, missy. You don't have to carry it yo'self."

"I'm trying, honestly. But it's so hard at times."

"I know it is, but don't you think it was hard on God when He let His Son die for the sins of this world? Ain't nuthin' that's worth anything that don't cost us something."

She'd recently read in the New Testament about how Jesus had willingly died on the cross to set man free from the bondage of sin. She thought of Millie's sweet baby and how hard it would be for her to sacrifice her child. Carina shook her head. It would be unbearable to watch your child suffer. How much more must it have been for God, who could have merely uttered a word or even a whisper and made all of His Son's suffering on the cross stop.

How small and petty her worries seemed in the light of Christ's sacrifice.

"Thank you, Abel. You sure are wise."

She made her way past the barn but paused when she saw the wagon in the yard. "Oh no. Not again." This was the third time since the day Johnny and Millie had arrived that William Dean had come to visit, and each time was just before the noon meal.

She was in no mood to see him again. He was a nice enough man—and his children were sweet—but she had no desire to marry him. How was she going to get that across to him?

Carina spun around and hurried past the barn. Abel's brows lifted when she came his way again, but she turned right and darted behind the barn. Lifting her skirts, she climbed into the paddock and hunkered down, hoping the fence rails might give her some cover. Comet whickered and walked her way. "No!" She swatted her hand in the air. His head jerked up, but he didn't take the hint and slowly wandered in her direction. Not wasting any more time on the gelding, she looked for Mr. Dean, and when she didn't see him, she made a mad dash toward the side of the house.

Etta sat outside the kitchen and saw her coming. "Wha'cha doin', Miz 'Rina?" she called out loudly.

"Shhh. . ." Carina held her finger to her lips.

Etta glanced around, eyes wide. "What's wrong? How come we gotta be quiet?"

Heaving a sigh, Carina straightened. What was the point of sneaking around when you had Etta to announce your presence?

As she crept in the back door, she thought she heard the front door close. Could she be so fortunate? She tiptoed past the stairway leading to the second floor and into the parlor, where she peeked out the front window. Sure enough, Mr. Dean was climbing into his wagon. He stood there a minute, hands on hips, and slowly turned in a half circle. Was he looking for her?

He turned back toward the front of the house, and she jumped sideways, out of view. Holding her breath, she listened for the jingle of harnesses, and then finally let the air from her lungs.

"What in the world are you doin' standing in the corner, child?"

Carina jumped. How could a woman as large as Betsey be so quiet when she wanted to be?

"I ain't seen you doin' that since. . .well. . .can't say as I ever have."

"You scared me."

"What are you up to?" Her maid narrowed her eyes. "Hiding. Mmm-hmm. From that nice Mr. Dean. Shame on you."

Yes, he was nice, but he wasn't Reed Bishop, and she didn't want to give the man any false hopes.

"Well, never you mind. Yo' daddy's wantin' to see you. That lawyer man was here whilst you was out checkin' the fields." Betsey's wide grin reached from ear to ear. "So get on up there. I'm dyin' to hear the good news."

Had he finally changed his will to make her his heir? Dare she hope? But what else could her fader want? He never asked for her, not unless he wanted to try again to get her to buy him some whiskey, but even those requests had come less often of late. Standing outside his door, she braced herself. In spite of Betsey's optimism, she had a feeling she wouldn't like what he was going to say.

She rapped on his door then pushed it open. The room was darker than usual with all but one of the curtains shut tight. The stench and the heat were nearly unbearable. How did he stand it? She swallowed hard. "You wanted to see me?"

"I did. Here." He flung a half-curled piece of parchment paper at her.

Unrolling it, she tilted it toward the light and read the heading. *Last Will and Testament.*

She sucked in a breath and glanced at her fader. This was it. He must have changed his mind. Why else would he have her read his will? Her gaze dropped back to the paper, and she scanned the information. Her heart stopped.

I will my complete estate to my son, Johan Karl Zimmer, and in the event of his death to his legal heirs.

"I don't understand. Why would you leave everything to a son who is dead?"

Her fader's eyes gazed past her, to the right.

"Because he isn't dead."

She spun around, hand on her chest, at the sound of a man's voice coming from the corner. Johnny stepped out of the shadows, wearing a shirt that had belonged to her brother, a shirt that hung far too loose on his skeletal frame. He had shaved and washed his hair. He resembled someone, but who? She shoved the thought away. "What are you doing in Fader's room?"

A smirk lifted his lips on one side. "You don't even recognize your own brother? You disappoint me, Carina."

"Johan?" She studied his features. He had matured and

looked far different. He'd always been thin, but his cheeks had never been hollow. When he reached up and tugged on his ear, she knew it was him. "How is it you're alive? You died."

"I'm sorry, but it is me."

She didn't know whether to run and embrace the brother she'd missed so much or not. He made no move to come to her. In fact, he seemed colder than she remembered. Distant. How could she have not known him when she first saw him? "Now I know why you never let anyone see your face."

He shrugged, and the tiniest of grins pulled at one side of his mouth. A fire lit in her stomach. The brother she loved so much was home—back from the grave. God had truly worked a miracle for her. She stepped toward him. "Don't I get a hug? Remember how you used to fall into my skirts and embrace my legs?"

He frowned, looking much like her fader, who remained oddly quiet. "Let's wait until you've heard everything and see if you still want one."

She reached back and grabbed hold of the footboard again. What could that mean? "At least explain how it is that you're alive."

That grin again, as if he had pulled something off on everyone. "I was never hurt as bad as you assumed."

"But I saw the blood."

"What you saw was a red wine stain and *some* blood."

Behind her, her fader chuckled, as if he'd been part of the ruse.

She concentrated hard, trying to remember that awful day. Was it possible? She'd been so distraught. Could she have missed such a thing? All she remembered was the blood. How pale he'd looked. How much pain he'd been in. "You tricked me?"

It must be true, for here he was. She lifted her gaze to his face, longing to touch him, to make certain she wasn't dreaming. "So why did you disappear? Where have you been?"

A muscle twitched in his jaw, and he scowled again. "What happened is that I fainted, Carina. I was so afraid when I shot Reed Bishop in the arm and he raised that pistol to shoot me, I simply fainted. He winged my side as I fell." He stared at the ground and shook his head. "All I'd ever been was a weakling who'd hung on his sister's skirts. I was too embarrassed to face anyone after that. I had to get away from here—get away from *you.*"

"Me?" A searing pain lanced her heart. Johan despised her as much as their fader did? "I—I don't understand. All I did was care for you—love you."

He huffed a haughty laugh. "Of course you don't. You smothered me. You were always the strong one, so strong that I never had a chance. Like the bigger baby bird that forces the smaller one from the nest."

His words blistered a spot deep within that her fader had never been able to reach. The boy she'd loved so much hated her, and she still didn't understand why. She loved him as much as a mother loved her own child. She hung her head, wanting just to flee the room.

"I had an interesting visitor a short while ago," her fader said, his voice as haughty as her brother's. "Mr. Dean, a fine man if I do say so, has asked to marry you, and I've agreed."

"No!" She clutched the bed frame with both hands. "You can't. I don't love him."

"Ha! What does that matter?"

She tightened her grip on the wood bars, trying hard to stay upright. "Why? All I ever did was take care of this place.

To make sure we kept our land when you took to your bed. I've worked dawn to dusk to make sure we all have food to eat. Why are you doing this?"

He sat up, his eyes cold. "Because you sought to replace me. Thought you could run this place on your own, and look at it. You've sold three-fourths of our land."

It was only one-fourth, but she didn't have the strength to correct him. She was losing the one thing she held dear: Tanglewood.

"You sold my slaves and pocketed the money and refused to buy me whiskey. You chased my only son and heir away and made friends with my mortal enemy. It's not one thing, it's many that you've done. Now do you understand?"

He didn't want an answer. His mind was made up.

"Tanglewood belongs to your brother now. Pack up your things and prepare to leave. Mr. Dean will be by to collect you at noon tomorrow."

Numb. Cold. As if her blood had thickened, Carina could hardly move. She forced herself to turn, keeping one hand on the bed frame. Lifting her gaze to Johan, she hoped to see a speck of the boy she'd cherished, but he was not there. He'd been replaced by a coldhearted imposter. His arms were crossed over his thin chest, and the look on his face said *checkmate*.

Somehow she made it to the hall. Millie's door was open, and she was bent over the bed, talking to her son. How ironic that Carina had placed them in the room that had been Johan's. She realized that the woman she was staring at was her sister-in-law. The baby was her nephew. But she knew in her heart that he would never know her.

Tears filled her eyes and overflowed. She sucked in a sob. Millie turned, giving her a curious stare. She stood and smiled, started to come to her. In that moment, Carina was certain that she didn't know of her husband's deception.

She raced down the hall, ignoring Millie's calls, turned into her room, and locked the door. Sliding down to the floor, the floodgates burst. She had lost everything.

Reed.

Her family.

Her home.

But most of all, the slaves—her dear friends.

Now she fully understood what it must feel like to be a slave, torn asunder from all that one loved.

nineteen

"Let's call off this whole thing, Mother." Reed buttoned his Highland frock coat, knowing his request would not be granted. His mother had invited half of Charleston to tonight's ball, while he had no desire to see a soul.

"You know it's too late. And seeing all your friends and our business associates will be good for you. Maybe it will pull you out of your melancholy."

She was wrong. He paced to the window and looked down on the carriages coming up the drive like ants to a picnic. Several servants were directing the guests where to park. How would he make it through this long afternoon and evening? He'd be expected to smile and dance. How could he make merry when his heart was shattered?

The woman he loved was married.

Why hadn't he acted sooner? Tried again to reason with her stubborn father?

He'd gone to check on his patients two days ago—to tell Carina he loved her, but she was already gone. Gone with William Dean. Reed clamped down on his back teeth. Hadn't she known his heart? Why had she been in such a hurry to marry?

She must have had feelings for Will. That was the only answer he could come up with.

"Come, now. We must greet our guests."

He clung to the window ledge. *Help me get through this night, Lord. Then help me through tomorrow. And the next day.*

My heart is empty. Deflated.

His mother tugged on his arm. "Come. You're the host tonight."

He hung his head. "I can't. Go without me."

She raised her arms, cupping his cheeks with her warm hands. "Look at me, Reed."

He managed to do as she asked, but even that took effort.

"Now, listen to me. You have to trust God. You can't give up."

"I don't know how to go on without her. She was the brave one. The one with heart."

"What you say about Carina is true, but don't cut yourself short. You're a talented, godly man with a heart of gold. God has plans for you, but if you wallow in self-pity, you'll be worthless to Him." She gave him a gentle shake. "You've got to trust Him. Do you understand?"

He closed his eyes, letting the truth of her words soak in. Since he had lost Carina, he'd all but walked away from God. His hurt had kept him away. *I'm sorry, Father. Please forgive me. Strengthen me.* "I hear you, Mother."

"Good, and it's *Mama*. Now let's go."

❧

She didn't want to come, but William had insisted—been quietly adamant and unrelenting—so unlike him.

How could she face Reed? Face all the others who had to be whispering about her. And what if Johan and Millie came? Surely Susan wouldn't have invited them, and yet they were her neighbors now.

She'd dawdled so long that they'd missed the meal, but she didn't care. That just meant less time at Reed Springs. She stood against one wall, attempting to hide behind a trio of plants. She had only seen Reed a time or two when he passed by dancing with a pretty woman, but each time it had been a different woman. Did he ever think of her these days?

The fast-paced music of the Cally polka slowed and the musicians shifted to a slower-paced waltz. That was one more dance completed. A few more minutes until they could leave.

"Excuse me, ma'am, but could I have this dance?"

Reed. Carina sucked in a sharp breath, afraid to move. How could she say yes? How could she touch him? Be so close as to feel his breath on her cheek? To look into his eyes? She kept her head down and shook it. "I'm sorry. I can't."

"Why, would your *husband* object?"

The bitterness in his voice drew up her head. "Husband?"

Reed's gaze hardened to a smoky blue. "Will's not here tonight? Surely you didn't come without an escort. Why, that would be as scandalous as riding a horse astride."

Why was he deliberately trying to provoke her? "I—"

She couldn't stand there and not touch him. Not see the fire ignite in his gaze when he looked at her. This Reed Bishop was not a man she knew. Pivoting sideways, she darted between two of the plants and raced outside. Unlike the last dreadful ball she'd attended, this one took place on the second floor of the Reed home. She ran onto the piazza and found herself trapped with no place to go. At least she didn't have to look at him. She gazed out on the beautiful garden below. The azaleas flamed bright pink, red, and white, while a myriad of other flowers turned their faces to the sun that would soon be setting.

Her heart pounded at the deliberate footsteps slowly coming her way. What did he want her to say? That she was sorry for what her fader had said to him? He had no idea how truly sorry she was.

He blew out a heavy sigh. "I'm sorry, Carina. I so wanted things to be different."

She blinked her eyes, trying hard to keep from crying. Her throat ached. What torture this was.

"Have you nothing to say?"

From the corner of her eye, she saw him rub the arm that had been wounded in the duel. At that moment she realized how she'd wronged him. "I'm so sorry, Reed."

"For what?"

She had to look at him when she apologized. She owed him that much. Lifting her gaze to his, her heart clenched. There was so much pain it nearly buckled her knees. "I'm sorry for blaming you for Johan's death. I'm sure you've heard by now that he's alive and well and living at Tanglewood."

"Yes, I did, but I don't know whether to congratulate you or offer condolences."

She had to smile at that. "Considering all that's happened, I'd say condolences is probably the correct choice."

His hands lifted to her upper arms. The light breeze lifted his hair then dropped it. "What did happen?"

"What have you heard?"

"Not much. When I rode over to check on Abel, he was the only one I saw, and he didn't say much. Just that nothing was the same with you gone."

Her lower lip quivered. "I miss them all so much." She lost the battle against her tears.

His gaze softened. "I didn't mean to make you cry." He lifted his thumbs, and ever so softly wiped her tears with them.

The music drifted out the open doors, as if calling them to take part. Reed's finger slid up her temple and lifted her hair, revealing the row of sutures. "I need to come by and take those out, probably this week. Do you think your husband would mind?"

Hadn't he said that before? "I don't have a husband."

His hand stilled, as did his breathing. His eyes dropped to hers. "What about Will?"

She shook her head. "We aren't married yet."

"But you're living at his place."

"But I'm not living *with* him."

Reed stepped closer. "Then where?"

She ducked her head. Will had agreed only as long as she didn't tell anyone, but she couldn't hurt Reed further by lying to him. She shrugged and offered a weak smile. "He fixed up one of the old slave cabins on his farm. He doesn't own any slaves, so I have the whole place to myself."

Reed closed his eyes as if the thought pained him, but the next words out of his mouth shocked her. "Thank You, Lord!"

She pulled away. "You're happy I'm living like a slave? Not that it's all that bad where I am."

He instantly sobered. "No, I'm not happy about that at all. Why *are* you living there?"

"You're serious. You really don't know?"

He shook his head. "I rode over to Tanglewood, ready to defy your father and to confess how much I love you, but Johan said that you had married Will Dean. I can't really tell you what happened after that. All I knew was I'd lost you."

Carina held her breath. Dare she believe it possible? "Do you really? Love me?"

He cupped her cheeks and touched her forehead to his. "With all my heart. Don't marry Will. Please, Carina. I don't know how to go on with my life if you're not in it, by my side. I need your strength."

She sucked back a sob and fell into his arms. Abel had been right when he'd told her to trust God to work things out. Carina felt as if she'd finally come home. Home in Reed

Bishop's arms. He pulled back and gazed on her face, all the love he felt flowing from his amazing eyes—eyes she hoped their children would one day have.

He leaned down, touching his lips to hers, sealing his pledge of love.

A woman cleared her throat, and Carina jumped back from Reed.

"Mother?"

"I see you two have reconciled things." Susan smiled. "Are you having a good time?"

Carina glanced at Reed, whose ears had flamed as red as her heart.

"Yes, Mother, we're having a fabulous time."

"Wonderful. I just wanted to let you know that Mr. Dean has returned home."

Reed blinked. "What do you mean?"

Susan's head lifted, a smug smile on her pretty face. "He and I had a discussion the other day when I delivered the gown to Carina. I let him know that she was spoken for, even if she didn't know it yet."

"Mother!"

If Carina had any doubts that Reed knew of his mother's talk with Will, the forcefulness in the single word drove it away.

Susan held up her palm, as if to silence her son. "You may thank me later, Reed. Right now a certain young lady awaits your attention." She turned back to the door.

"Mother!"

Glancing over her shoulder, she tossed them a satisfied grin.

"It's *Mama*—to both of you."

A Letter To Our Readers

Dear Reader:

In order that we might better contribute to your reading enjoyment, we would appreciate your taking a few minutes to respond to the following questions. We welcome your comments and read each form and letter we receive. When completed, please return to the following:

Fiction Editor
Heartsong Presents
PO Box 719
Uhrichsville, Ohio 44683

1. Did you enjoy reading *Dueling Hearts* by Vickie McDonough?
   ❏ Very much! I would like to see more books by this author!
   ❏ Moderately. I would have enjoyed it more if

   _____

   _____

   _____

2. Are you a member of **Heartsong Presents**? ❏ Yes ❏ No
   If no, where did you purchase this book? _____

   _____

3. How would you rate, on a scale from 1 (poor) to 5 (superior), the cover design? _____

4. On a scale from 1 (poor) to 10 (superior), please rate the following elements.

   ____ Heroine   ____ Plot
   ____ Hero   ____ Inspirational theme
   ____ Setting   ____ Secondary characters

5. These characters were special because? _____

_____

_____

6. How has this book inspired your life? _____

_____

_____

7. What settings would you like to see covered in future
   Heartsong Presents books? _____

_____

_____

8. What are some inspirational themes you would like to see
   treated in future books? _____

_____

_____

9. Would you be interested in reading other **Heartsong
   Presents** titles?   ❑ Yes   ❑ No

10.   Please check your age range:
      ❑ Under 18   ❑ 18-24
      ❑ 25-34   ❑ 35-45
      ❑ 46-55   ❑ Over 55

Name _____

Occupation _____

Address _____

City, State, Zip _____